FLIGHT OF THE CONDOR

AIR PIRATES OF CYRENAICA
BOOK TWO

BLAZE WARD

KNOTTED ROAD PRESS

ALSO BY BLAZE WARD

The Jessica Keller Chronicles

Auberon

Queen of the Pirates

Last of the Immortals

Goddess of War

Flight of the Blackbird

The Red Admiral

St. Legier

Winterhome

Petron

CS-405

Queen Anne's Revenge

Packmule

Persephone

First Centurion Kosnett

Encounter at Vilahana

Consensus at Aditi

Hegemony at Dalou

Princes at Ewin

Empire at Gloran

Domain at Yaumgan

Additional Alexandria Station Stories

The Story Road

Siren

Two Bottles of Wine With A War God

The Science Officer Series Season One

The Science Officer

The Mind Field

The Gilded Cage

The Pleasure Dome

The Doomsday Vault

The Last Flagship

The Hammerfield Gambit

The Hammerfield Payoff

The Bryce Connection

The Science Officer Series Season Two

Alien Seas

Buried Among the Stars

Captain Navarre

Last Stand

Lost Dreams

Ghost Towns

Games People Play

Hard Bargain

Outermost

Dominion-427

Phoenix

Princess Rualoh

MEDITERRANEAN SEA
BENGHAZI
ACRE
PALESTINE
JORDAN
LIBYA
EGYPT
CAIRO
HEJAZ
KHARGA
RED SEA
JABAL AL
UWAYAT

CHAPTER ONE

"Okay. So let me make sure I understand all this," Finn said as he walked around the aircraft. Something about possession of stolen goods. Things might be getting a little messy at some point. "You are seriously telling me that this thing fell off the back of a truck?"

Finn knew his Montana drawl came out something hard in times like this. Made him probably sound like something of a yokel to this fine, Cairo gentleman who looked an awful lot like a pickpocket who had graduated up to larceny and maybe grand theft. Even as they had all traveled up to Alexandria for this next adventure.

"Indubitably, Mr. Severijns," Magdy the Arms Merchant replied, bowing ever so slightly in the way of an Egyptian arms dealer and smuggler. His voice had the kind of greasiness to it that almost made Finn want to take another shower. He'd already shaved today. "They were boxed up in Germany for shipment to China. As to why the aircraft was lost here, I cannot even begin to guess. However, when my friend came to me and asked about the possibility of you selling your current aircraft and perhaps desiring to trade up, we were able to make a most lucrative deal to have the plane unboxed from where it had been stored then assembled and prepped for flight."

Finn turned to one of his companions now and studied him.

The Man With No Face, as he was generally known in the souqs and slums of Cairo. He actually had a name. Several, depending on how you wanted to interpret that. Generally, he answered to Asher.

Short for *Autonomous Simulated Human Exploration Robot.*

Fellow was an alien machine in the rough shape of a man. Claimed all his flesh had been burned off in the crash that originally stranded him on Earth in 1916.

Any of you fellows want to buy a bridge?

Except he'd seen Asher without that heavy, flowing robe that the man—creature?—habitually wore. Or the turban, gloves, pants, and boots. Without that pretty, enameled mask he wore to make everyone else think he was another one of those poor survivors of the Great War who'd suffered such terrible damage that the mask hid his scars.

Finn knew a lot of boys like that.

None of them were aluminum pipes connected with ball joints.

Still, Asher was good people. Even if he wasn't people.

"And you trust all this?" Finn asked the man, gesturing to all of the everything involved.

"Indeed, Finn," Asher replied. "I have known Magdy for many years, and found him to be an honest and reliable chap."

The English accent that came out of his mask's mouth

hole, with just a touch of Egyptian crispness, didn't help Finn's humor, but if Asher was willing to vouch for the smuggler, that said a lot.

Finn still owed Asher for a couple of big things.

Speaking of...

Finn turned the other side with a generic shrug, letting his eyes fall on the woman who was his boss. More or less.

Employer of record, at a minimum, if they all ended up getting arrested at some point.

Zareen Vüsala Shirazi.

She was short, around five foot four. Nice ass, shown off today in dove gray jodhpurs. No chest to speak of under that white linen shirt and matching gray vest. Average enough waist. Long black hair pulled back into a braid.

The face was what stopped traffic, if she wanted to. All the best parts from her Scots/English father and Persian princess mother. Brains from both of them, too. Money as well. Twenty-two years old, near as Finn could tell. Young enough to be his daughter, which was fine.

He preferred looking at her bodyguard, Ghada. That woman was curvier, but it was all muscle. With really cute dimples when she chose to smile.

Ghada was sort of smiling right now, but it was more trying to keep a straight face than anything. Finn felt like he was the straight man in someone else's joke.

Everyone else's joke.

"So," Finn addressed himself to Zareen. "How many countries do you currently have arrest warrants out?"

Kinda priceless, watching the way that cool, aristocratic mien suddenly scrunched up in confusion like she'd just sucked a lemon.

"What are you talking about, Finn?" she asked.

The face screamed Persian nobility pretty enough for Hollywood, had she wanted. The voice was pure London, even posher than the nice ladies on the World Service at night.

Ghada did smile now. So did Hans, Finn's original mechanic back when it was just the two of them and *Cerberus*, the old Ford Trimotor he was apparently in the process of selling or trading for this new aircraft.

The one that had fallen off the back of a truck, somewhere between Hamburg and Cairo, far short of Peking where it was originally destined.

Not that Finn knew *anything* at all about the delicate art of smuggling and fencing stolen goods. All those years in and around Chicago were just him flying interesting businessmen to meetings. Or delivering priority air cargoes that often had to land at night on unlit runways, to be met by folks in such a hurry that they just unloaded boxes out of the boots of cars as they drove up.

Y'all wanna buy a bridge?

"Warrants. If we do this," Finn smiled at her. "And I'm not saying no, mind you. But if we do this, there's going to have to be some fast tap dancing at some point. A Heinkel HE-111 bomber's kinda hard to miss. Even if we tell folks that it is the 111-C model for civilian traffic. Don't matter what kind of paint job we slap on it. Most of them are accounted for already."

"Uhm." Hans chose to get involved now, the big Kraut always a stickler for those sorts of details. "Luft Hansa has a bunch of older ones, some of which aren't in service anymore. Plus a few that the Condor Legion lost in Spain, pretty early in the war. And, of course, six that never made it to China, for reasons best not explored in a public place."

"Why are warrants a topic, Finn?" Zareen asked.

"Ain't nobody in Egypt that currently wants to arrest me," Finn smiled proudly. "Obviously, nobody has caught up yet. If I'm flying around in a slightly stolen German bomber, even one configured as a civilian transport, someone's going to ask questions. Might arrest the lot of us on general principle and then start poking at your story."

He didn't like necessarily dragging this out in front of the arms merchant, but Asher had vouched for the man. And they could always drag him down, too, if someone decided to arrest them for possession of stolen goods like this. Finn could always tell them who he bought the plane from.

Still, Finn was hopeful that Zareen had the sorts of contacts with the British Army and others that might smooth things over.

"Oh," she replied, obviously surprised. Her eyes went wide with sudden recognition.

Finn didn't get to do that to Zareen that often. Woman was too damned smart for her own good. But there was book smarts, like Zareen Shirazi had, and Cairo slums smart.

That was Asher's department. Of course, he didn't officially exist, so that might cause a few raised eyebrows with the stuffy twits of High Command, but Finn was just an employee.

Zareen was the spy.

However, it was fun to watch her face pale a little under that Persian hue. The eyes got a little flustered, glancing sidelong at Magdy the arms merchant.

The fifth member of the group stepped up now. He'd been staying a little back during all this, since he wasn't official or anything. Just another Senussi warlord from the

Libyan interior visiting relatives in Egypt. A prince of some sort himself, also half-blood, with bright blue eyes.

Emad al-Sadri. Good fellow. Guerrilla fighting the same Italians Finn had taken a hankering to hassling. And maybe Emad was also courting Zareen some, but minding his manners about it. Finn and Hans would see to that, not that it should be a problem.

"I can also make a few inquiries," Emad said, cerulean eyes boring in on Magdy. "Perhaps cousin Idris can provide some documentation."

Cousin Idris. Who might have become king of Libya, or at least Cyrenaica, without those stupid fascists from Rome causing troubles o'er yonder for the last twenty-five years. Finn was fast enough to watch Magdy's face show a hint of panic as well.

Maybe y'all wandered into Affairs of State, buddy?

Finn smiled. Seemed to reassure folks, so that must be good.

"Tell you what," Finn turned to include everyone in that smile. "Let's take it up for a spin and see how she flies. Then we can make a decision."

"Excellent, Mr. Severijns," Magdy smiled all grease and butter, if still a touch pale. "I look forward to your report when you return."

"Oh, no, Magdy," Finn's smile turned feral. "Yer coming with us."

CHAPTER TWO

Zareen listened as the engines began to roar, but she could not decide if this air frame was louder than *Cerberus*. The plane could be crowded, but it was configured for civilian usage, so nobody had mounted the guns in the dorsal, ventral, or lateral turrets.

Not yet, at least.

She was comfortable now in what would have been the bomb bay, configured currently as a four-seat "smoking compartment," with another six seats behind her in the rear fuselage.

Finn and Hans were up front flying. Well, taxiing and getting a running start at the sky. Ghada, her bodyguard, was seated where the dorsal gunner/radio operator would be, leaving her with Asher, Emad, and Magdy.

Zareen could see either removing these four seats, or possibly the other six, for future adventures. Hans had muttered something about load displacements, so she wasn't sure which would have to go, but Zareen didn't foresee carrying a bomb load and needing to blow someone up anytime soon.

That wasn't the same as not doing it. She glanced over at Emad with a subtle grin.

His face asked a question, but the noise was too loud, even as the big Heinkel was aloft finally and climbing with a smooth roar that was less disconcerting than the way *Cerberus* did it.

Magdy seemed to be reading her mind, or perhaps her expression.

"Would there be a future interest in changing the internal configurations of the aircraft, assuming you went ahead with the purchase?" he asked with enough of a yell and lean in as to be clear.

Emad's face lit up for a moment before it got smooth and cagey again.

Yes, two weeks ago, the man had never flown in an airplane, being a leader of a small group of Senussi warriors down in the southern deserts where Cyrenaica, Egypt, and Sudan intersected. Rebels resisting the Italian invasion.

Finn and Hans had already changed his life by repairing that Italian armored car they'd stolen, out in the desert, allowing those folks to launch more dangerous raids than before, as well as leaving them all the spare gasoline Finn hadn't needed to get home.

Idris of Cyrenaica had then given Emad his personal blessing to turn over command of that warband to another cousin, with the understanding that Emad's new friends were quite interested in doing hostility unto the Italians.

Zareen had nothing personal against Mussolini, but she knew that Finn and Hans were still sore at the way they had been treated: fired and abandoned while in the air on the way to Cairo and left to fend for themselves. Plus, the Italians were making noises about moving beyond what they had done to Abyssinia already this summer.

The two men had kept the plane *Cerberus* as a result. Some might suggest stolen it, but possession was a point of order. And they might be about to trade it for a stolen German bomber masquerading as a civilian air liner.

"How hard would such a reconfiguration be?" Zareen asked, once it was obvious that Emad would not speak. She turned her attention to the odd man out.

Magdy shrugged eloquently.

"The parts are not currently available in any warehouse that I am familiar with," he said. "However, as Mr. Fertig pointed out earlier, the nationalists lost several aircraft in Spain, as well as having parts stored there for the Condor Legion to use. I'm sure something could be accomplished."

Zareen glanced at Asher, but she knew the alien would not counsel such a course of action. His programming forbade him from injuring humans, except as a terminal recourse.

Randomly bombing Italian troops would not likely ever rise to that level. She had spoken privately with the machine man enough to understand that. Similarly, Emad had desires on the topic, but would not speak them at present.

It would be entirely her decision. Even Finn would accept that. Hans just tended to go along with things, happy to keep the aircraft, either of them, ready to fly.

Still, Asher had surprised her by spending his own money to get this craft operational, even before her group reached the conclusion to buy it. *Cerberus* was a lovely plane, but it was already nearly a decade old, in an era where it seemed that a revolution in aircraft occurred every spring.

That Asher was willing to contribute funds to this as well, for reasons he had not explained, still spoke volumes.

Finn and Hans had no money, save for selling the stolen *Cerberus*. Emad as well, although he could likely tap external resources from the hidden Court of his cousin.

Even Zareen did not have that much money on her own, but the British authorities who secretly supported her had been willing to get quietly involved when she mentioned all this to them.

Anyone preventing a stolen German bomber from falling into unfriendly hands probably passed muster with the British Army, all things considered.

"Magdy," she said, after balancing her scales. "I do not foresee us needing to make that change immediately, but let us suppose that external events may be thrust upon us in the future."

She shared a knowing nod with the fellow. Italy now had colonies on either side of British Egypt. And Mussolini was not particularly subtle with his future intentions.

Another Great War loomed, but nobody knew when it would arrive, or what form it would take, save that the Axis Powers of Germany, Italy, and Japan would become a threat to everyone, everywhere.

"Let us suppose," the man agreed with a nod. "I will make a few inquiries when I return to Cairo. May I presume that you are not likely to be in Cairo in the immediate future?"

"That would be wise," Asher spoke up now. "But I have ways of getting messages to you as needed."

Zareen didn't inquire. Asher had lived in secret in the Cairo slums for more than twenty years now. Of course, he had options.

"Finn," she called now as the aircraft seemed to be leveling off. He had surprised her by not flying out over the sea, but she supposed that if something went wrong, it would be better not to have to swim. Asher would sink like a stone.

However, the noise still precluded conversation, so she unbuckled and rose, gesturing the others to remain here. If they did buy this, she could see the need for an intercom linking this area with the cockpit.

Making her way forward, she joined Finn and Hans, admiring the view out the front glass.

"Ma'am?" Finn asked, turning to look at her.

"Should we?" she asked back, gesturing around them. "Does this aircraft meet your needs?"

"Absolutely," Finn nodded, glancing over and getting a nod from Hans as well. "But does it meet yours?"

"What do you mean?"

"I don't figure we're going to stay put in Alexandria," Finn continued. "Or run back and forth hauling supplies to Emad's friends. What could we do with a stolen German bomber before anybody knows we got it?"

Zareen rocked back on her heels and wondered. She had the element of surprise at the moment, since nobody would be able to anticipate her. How should she employ that for greatest advantage?

"Hans, how do you feel about returning to your homeland?" she pressed, slightly evasively.

He turned and gave her a droll, almost angry look.

Hans Fertig was German. In the Great War, he had been

a motor pool mechanic who'd learned to repair aircraft. Like the American Finn, he had drifted after the war, but staying in planes, until he had been paired up with Finn as the flight crew for Aurora Italian Airlines in one of those random acts of chance that had the potential to alter the future, at least as Zareen saw it.

The two men had become fast friends and blood brothers.

She fixed Hans with her own hard look in response.

"And how would you feel about playing an enormous practical joke on the Luftwaffe, while making the Italians look even more inept that normal?" she continued, breaking into a smile.

"*Das ist gut*," he rumbled back at her. "Perhaps troublesome, but good."

"Zareen, how would we go about getting the Kraut here new papers?" Finn spoke up. "American, or maybe Swiss citizenship? If things are going to get rough, he needs to be protected, especially if war is coming and your British authorities decide to lock everyone up first and only start asking questions afterward."

Zareen nodded, lips pursed. It was a cogent question.

"Let me inquire," she said. "But I will go ahead and effect the sale of *Cerberus* and purchase of this aircraft, if you approve."

"Yeah, do that," Finn said. "Looking forward to what you have in mind."

Zareen made her way aft and smiled at the assembled company.

"Magdy, I believe we can execute a sales contract," she said with a nod and a smile that encompassed them all. "In addition, I have some other tasks that I think you would be quite well suited to performing for us afterwards, for something I would like to do next."

"Madame?" he asked, eyes wide open with interest.

So she told him, watching the group erupt with mirth as she did.

CHAPTER THREE

Asher had his qualms about the undertaking, but he could not argue with the humanity behind it. At least he had learned that much about the species over the last twenty-three Earth years.

Fascists notwithstanding, they could be as warm and helpful to one another as the Durren who had originally constructed him. Even if the planet itself was still hostile and humans still categorized as a Class Red species, to be isolated from galactic culture by all means until they reached a level of adult sophistication that would allow them to safely interact.

The impending sequel to the prior European Great War, however, would be larger, deadlier, and more reinforcing of that Class Red status.

As the aircraft circled back and began to approach the runway for landing, Asher considered what he had learned.

Aristocracy as a governing ideology had largely given way over the last century, with republican forms of government frequently replacing them. The one benefit of the Great War had been to finally shatter the hold of the last major monarchs ruling by divine right, with Germany, Turkey, and Austro-Hungary no longer even Empires. Russia as well, but he had not been able to determine if the efforts of Comrade Stalin had markedly improved things for his citizens.

Fascism, however, had not been an improvement, from the standpoint of an Autonomous Simulated Human Exploration Robot, even one that could no longer adequately simulate a human, with all his organic flesh burned off in the crash that had permanently stranded him on this planet. The fascist leaders appeared to be at least as bad as the kings and emperors they had replaced.

Still, his mission had not changed. He still sought to learn about humans and come to understand their culture well enough to explain it to the Durren.

Hopefully, they would salvage his datacore and all he had learned, if they ever did return and arrest him.

"Why fascism?" he turned to Zareen Shirazi and asked her.

This woman struck him in the top few percentage points of intelligence, for all the humans he had encountered over the last generation.

He had, however, confused her now.

"Why is fascism such a seductive song for your various cultures at present?" Asher continued, expanding the question, realizing that even robots can get lost in their own internal circuits.

"Ah," she said, pausing to order her thoughts before replying.

Yet another reason he valued the woman and had chosen to ally himself with her, when it had become obvious that he could no longer hide from the outside world.

Emad al-Sadri and Magdy the arms merchant also seemed to lean into the conversation, as did Ghada Attar.

"The old world has crumpled," Zareen replied. "Those cultures held out as long as they could, so the eventual failure was both explosive and crippling. In my England, for example, or Finn's America, they spent an entire century moving away from aristocracy and developing other options. When everyone else lost the Great War, their cultures did not have the necessary strictures put into place that prevented things from going bad."

"And yet the Great Depression has gripped everyone, rich and poor alike," Asher noted.

"It has, but the American Hoover was proven desperately wrong, and Roosevelt replaced him," she continued. "In Britain, Baldwin and MacDonald have traded mandates now with differing views as to how to keep the system itself intact. Both countries have strong governmental systems larger than the men intent on dominating them. The others did not have that, so charismatic charlatans like Mussolini or Hitler could twist the system to benefit them, often by promising, as Mussolini did, to make the trains run on time. To make people's lives better, if they just gave up all control to the government."

"And that is a failure, if I read you correctly?" Asher asked.

He would have furrowed his brow, had he one still, so he had to resonate his voice instead.

"Neither of those men might be voted out of power, sirrah," she said tartly. "There is thus nothing that will moderate their behavior. Instead, I expect that their egos will continue to grow, along with their appetites, until they engulf us all in another cataclysm."

"And what you plan will have an effect on that?" he pressed.

"No," Zareen Shirazi surprised him by answering. "There is remarkably little I can do to thwart the forces growing. This project is something I can do for my friends, to make their lives better. And maybe help lift their spirits when the war does come."

"To paraphrase the Frenchman Bonaparte: *In war, moral power is to physical as three parts to one,*" Asher noted.

"Just so, my friend," she nodded. "I can make the world a slightly better place, and do something to discomfort my enemies."

"And that other Frenchmen?" Asher asked. "Beauchêne?"

As a sociologist, Asher appreciated the disdainful sneer that came over the woman's face. He had a similar opinion of the man, but that was a result of having scanned all of the human's notes, observations, ideas, and plans going back over five years when he broke into the man's hotel room.

"He is a thwarted pipsqueak," Zareen pronounced. "A bantam peacock fool of terribly small dreams, who seeks to find some magical formula or weapon that would allow him to cast down the Third Republic in France and replace it with some manner of fascist Reich that apes Hitler, bringing the debauched French to his way of thinking. I resist him as well. He is as bad as the various Nazis intent on their Teutonic, Aryan mysticisms that they think will grant them immortality and domination."

"You will stop him?" Asher asked, noting that Magdy was hardly breathing as he listened, but the man was as honest as any crooked purveyor of stolen goods and rumors might be.

And perhaps he also could be brought around to the right side of history, given time.

Asher had nothing but time, considering that his atomic reactor should have enough fuel at present consumption rates to outlive everyone on this aircraft. Plus the rising industrial technology suggested that he might be actually able to acquire the materials to refuel himself later.

On that date, he would need a smuggler whom he trusted.

"I will stop Beauchêne," Zareen agreed. "Or at least find and spread the technology he seeks so that I might neutralize him as a threat. I appreciate that you are an anthropologist and not an engineer, but hopefully there are things we can learn, various unknown technological secrets that will help the British and their allies resist the threat of fascism."

"It is good," Asher proclaimed.

He had chosen well.

Beauchêne was a bully, to use the human term. A man who gave no thought to the well-being of others, instead seeing them merely as objects to be exploited. Tools to be used up and discarded when they were no longer effective.

Zareen Shirazi cared about her friends. And tried to help complete strangers, in much the same way that Asher had quietly helped a number of children in Cairo's slums learn to read, against the day that they decided to rise up and free themselves from external domination.

That should not violate his programming, It might even weigh against his eventual judgment, when the Durren determined if the very crime of him existing balanced well against the things he had accomplished to help humans develop into a better species, after the ship that secretly brought him to Earth exploded and crashed.

Assuming that humans didn't shatter themselves and revert to a more primitive structure, having destroyed everything in their juvenile tantrums.

If they did, he would study that as well.

Outside, the wheels touched down and the plane began to taxi over to the hangar where it had been hidden before.

Asher turned to Magdy, his oldest ally in the souqs and slums of Cairo. The man had a beaming smile on his face.

"You agree with the next mission?" Asher asked.

"I am looking forward to it with glee, my old friend."

CHAPTER FOUR

Felt like it had been forever, but time had a way to doing that to a fellow.

Finn realized that it had been all of two weeks since he had left Cairo after rescuing Zareen and Ghada from that frog nemesis, Beauchêne. And the assassin known only as Bertrand.

Two weeks since he and Emad had walked into this very shop and gotten fancied up in nice suits by the polite Polish tailor, Mr. Kałuża. And then came back the next morning just long enough to trade the borrowed suits for better tailored ones.

Right before jumping in *Cerberus* and disappearing. If flying off to Port Said for a few days qualified. At least they'd gotten away from the Frenchie.

And now, snuck back into town in the back of a limousine, which had stopped just long enough for everyone to hop out and slip into Kałuża's shop.

Kinda crowded in here right now, but some things couldn't be helped.

"I don't know why I have to do this," Hans griped sourly, looking around.

"Because neither Finn nor Emad speak German fluently enough to fool anyone, Hans," Zareen answered from where she and Asher had taken seats off to one side.

Ghada was guarding the front door against anyone getting a little too nosy. Him, Emad, and the big kraut were standing in the middle of the room as the Pole measured the blond man.

"You do," Hans countered gruffly, but that was just him being him.

Any time he had to get out of the plane he was generally in a sour mood.

"And I will be accompanying you," Zareen nodded while Finn looked on and grinned. "However, you will need to appear as an officer capable of issuing orders to a pair of soldiers who are not expected to do much except follow them. Plus, you look the most German. Finn could possibly pass. And Emad's eyes will throw people off, but they are not tall, blond *Übermenschen, ja?*"

"*Ja,*" he replied with another grump.

"It is complete," Kałuża said as he stood and looked at them.

Apparently, the fussy, little man could hold all the numbers in his head, but he'd only looked at the two of them long enough apparently to make sure he still had everything from last time.

But Finn didn't figure he actually thought about flying. Just let his hands do things in a way that probably looked like magic to an outsider.

Maybe like tailoring.

"I grow concerned, madam," Kałuża addressed himself to

Zareen now, glancing at Asher and generally ignoring the others.

"At?" she asked, still seated and studying the man.

Kałuża turned now and gestured to Finn and the two men with him, about as Mutt and Jeff and Jeff as you could get, all things considered.

"Acquiring or constructing the necessary uniforms for the men will be easy enough, as the German embassy is close enough that I have done various tasks for them ere now," the tailor said. "Are you sure it is a wise course of action on your part to have uniforms of the German political forces made up? Under my understanding of things, that might cause you to be viewed as spies, rather than soldiers or even random mercenaries. The Germans lack a sense of humor."

"Dobie, I am willing to tell you the truth, as long as we understand that it must not be shared outside this room," Zareen said.

For being surrounded now by three big men, a robot, Ghada, and Zareen, the little man didn't even bother to react.

Imperturbable, as it were. Finn was impressed.

However, this was the same guy with expertise in tailoring men's suits for shoulder holsters and quick draw, so maybe he had seen his share of trouble over the years.

Finn didn't figure any European ever ended up in Egypt intentionally.

"Finn Severijns is selling his aircraft," Zareen said simply, gesturing his way. "The aircraft we are purchasing as a replacement is a German bomber that was apparently stolen at some point. With it, some planning, and a great deal of audacity, I believe we can simply fly into Bengasi and pretend to be Germans."

"To what end?" the little man demanded. "You are a

favored client and something of a friend, and I do not wish to see you killed for stupid or impractical reasons, Miss Shirazi."

"The Senussi still resist colonization by the Italians," she said, pointing now at Emad. "When they built the wire fence from the sea at Bardia to Jaghbub, two hundred and seventy kilometers inland, they were able to break that resistance, rounding up much of the population of Cyrenaica and putting them in camps, where terrible, staggering numbers of them subsequently died."

Finn had to give the fellow credit, he stood his ground and even shrugged, as if ignoring all of that because she hadn't answered his question.

Hadn't, as a matter of fact, but Finn trusted her.

"The Jebel Akhdar has been depopulated," she continued, really warming up to her subject now. Emad had helped prepare her, with his personal experience of much of that rebellion, before him and all his friends had been driven south.

"And what will you and your friends dressing up as Nazis do about that?" the tailor demanded, a chihuahua growling at a mountain lion.

"Some scholars from the university at Jaghbub are still in camps or prison, near Bengasi," she said. "Professors and learned men, whose crime consisted of not kowtowing to the fascists. Or perhaps not departing for Egypt in 1925 when the city was ceded."

"And?" Kałuża demanded.

"We're going to rescue them," Zareen said.

"Just like that?" Kałuża dismissed the idea, but he probably didn't understand the kind of woman he was dealing with.

Finn knew.

"Yes," she replied flatly. "Just like that."

CHAPTER FIVE

Didier Beauchêne felt like pulling his hair out, but outward bursts of emotion would do nothing to help the situation.

Instead, he sat calmly. Outwardly calmly at least. Listened to Bertrand's latest report. A cigarette burned in the ashtray, dying a slow, meaningless death like so many others before it. He must appear calm.

But even the killer's words were half-hearted.

"Something has changed," Didier said. "The streets have turned their hearts away from us."

"Acknowledged," Bertrand replied. "The information people are willing to share with me is slim, and the quality of rumors has dried up, but I am at a loss to understand what or why."

Didier processed the words the man had said. The reports of his investigations into the slums and neighborhoods of Cairo.

"All mention of The Man With No Face functionally ceased on the same day that we captured Zareen Shirazi and then lost her when her men rescued her," Didier stated.

A little light bulb would have gone on above his head, were this one of those American cartoons.

"Damn it," he snarled. "We have been approaching this as two, separate problems from the beginning. They are one."

"Monsieur?" Bertrand puzzled.

"How did the American and the other one find us so quickly that night?" Didier asked, almost rhetorically. "They had been back in Cairo for less than a day, and the other was just a Bedouin she brought back from wherever she had gone. How could they get to the warehouse almost as fast as we did?"

"They knew where it was," Bertrand replied slowly.

He was a fantastic killer, skilled the ways of mayhem and death, but strategic thinking was not the man's long suit.

"They knew where it was," Didier agreed. "Who told them?"

"Not me," the man recoiled as if accused.

Didier felt a moment of serene joy at the fear Bertrand had of him. Of his genius for inventing weapons and advanced technology.

"Not you," Didier agreed. "Who else might be interested in what we knew?"

"The Man With No Face," Bertrand replied automatically, still not making the connection.

"The same being who disappeared that night, never to be seen again," Didier said. "He must have told the American. And then joined forced with *that woman* and has been hiding behind her skirts since then. We must find the one to find the other."

"But why can we not find him?" Bertrand asked, still lost.

Linear thinking. The mark of a good killer. And a poor general.

"He has told all his contacts in Cairo to thwart us," Didier replied. "The Man With No Face has informed the underworld that we are enemies of his, and probably called in old favors."

"But how did he know where to find us?" Bertrand asked.

"Probably had people watching this very hotel," Didier shrugged. "They might still be, reporting your movements back to someone who passes the information on to one of our foes."

Didier rose now, automatically crushing out the crappy Turkish cigarette and buttoning his jacket. The room was large enough to pace.

"Someone has been watching us, but that should not have led them to the warehouse," he said. "Unless they had been in this very room."

A moment of pure panic electrified him.

"Move," Didier commanded the tall assassin as he approached the bed.

Bertrand rose, and Didier thrust a hand between the mattresses, locating his secret journal. That had mention of his plans, including that warehouse.

Someone had read it, he was sure. Some night, probably when he went to dinner, someone had broken into this very room and learned too much. Worse, they had done so in such a perfect manner that Didier had not had a hint until now.

He tossed the leather-bound journal onto the nearby desk with the others and turned his attention to the dresser.

Quickly, as Bertrand stood mutely nearby, Didier pulled out the second drawer, removed it entirely, and upended it on the bed, letting his clothing fall as it would. He didn't care.

Underneath he had taped an envelope. Ripping it loose, he opened the flap and unleashed a string of obscenities that should have summoned one of the old nuns with her ruler to smack his hand until it was raw and bloody.

"Didier?" Bertrand asked carefully.

"He has been here," the French industrialist snarled, turning and waving the envelope. "At one time, there was nearly one thousand English Pounds in here, Bertrand. Now, he has left me with fifty. Not enough to ruin this mission, but enough to send a message."

"What message?" the assassin asked.

"That it is time to play rough, as the Americans would say."

CHAPTER SIX

Zareen had been willing to hide in Alexandria, at least as much as they could, given the clubby confines of Egyptian society. It had been enough to bribe the hotel manager with a quick suggestion of a love affair gone wrong and the need to not be found, in order to have the man register them under Hans Fertig's name, even as she was paying.

Idly, she considered her earlier idea to return to the Persian highlands and recruit a small cadre of women like Ghada, all of them trained in the ancient combat ways of their ancestors. They almost reminded Zareen of the stories of geisha and ninjas from Nihon, deadly beautiful women assassins and entertainers.

All manner of interesting skills could be hidden within the concept of dance, if you wished. And lithe young women could easily distract, in a world so dominated by patriarchal blindness that they could never see a woman as a threat.

How she had lucked into the three men who currently worked for her was itself an amazing story.

One of them knocked at the door now. Right on time.

Ghada answered with a knife in one hand, hidden behind the door and ready to strike, as always.

Emad entered. Nervously, at that.

"You asked me to join you for tea?" he offered carefully.

Zareen smiled at the man. Tall and handsome, with a desert-lean body and blue eyes looking out from an otherwise Arabic face.

Another like her, born of two worlds and not really belonging to either. Also the child of palaces and diplomats, wealth and education.

How many others were there like the two of them? Were they the future of humanity, where everyone came together, or would the racialist tendencies of the fascists cause children like her and Emad al-Sadri to be hunted down?

"Please," Zareen gestured to the spare chair with a smile.

She could not risk being seen on the balcony, even with the fantastic view of the Mediterranean before her, so she was in the sitting room now, with the windows open to draw the ocean breeze and the sun just past directly overhead.

Emad sat in the other wingback chair, the two of them carefully separated by a small, round table upon which the tea would be placed.

Ghada was already heating water, having waited.

Zareen could have told her that Emad would be exactly on time. He and the other men shared that precision, going so far as to match their own watches at least twice daily.

She presumed it was a military thing, although Emad had never been anything but a guerrilla leader. He was too young to have fought in the Great War with the other men.

"The view is gorgeous, isn't it?" she asked, trying to put him more at ease.

He was twitchy. On the one hand, wishing to court her,

she knew, but held at some reserve by her background. Not many Senussi men probably met Persian princesses with a London accent and English education.

Plus, she knew that Finn and Hans watched the man like a hawk, protective uncles willing to step into the way if she found it necessary, but also willing to step back if she approved.

There were days Zareen wondered if she was living in some manner of bizarre fairy tale.

"Most lovely," he said ambiguously, looking more at her than the horizon.

Zareen smiled.

"Bengasi," she said simply, framing this as a military conversation, rather than courtship.

Not that she was opposed, but personal feelings could not get in the way of what she had taken on as her personal mission. All of the men who worked for her had a reason to dislike the Italians. With Emad, it went well beyond that, but even Finn was rather Red when pressed about his personal beliefs. Natural enemies of the fascists.

As was she, but for other reasons.

"Bengasi," he nodded, sobering instantly into the leader of a desert warband.

At least what he had been, before Idris, *that Idris*, had instructed Karim al-Sadri, an older cousin, to take charge, freeing up Emad for *other tasks*. Zareen had read the letter from the Emir of Cyrenaica to his cousin approving things.

Affairs of State, as Finn had noted dryly at one point.

"Most of your people who could have fled to Siwa or deep into the southern deserts," Zareen continued. "But many remained and were rounded up in camps on the coast."

"Yes," he agreed simply, but she could smell the anger wafting off the man.

How many of his friends or relatives had died as a result of the Italians and their grand plans?

"I cannot do anything for those," she continued, gentling her voice. "But you have told me of a handful that are still imprisoned. Those, I would rescue from captivity."

"Why?" he asked, nodding to accept everything she had just said but stepping over that and onto the deeper questions.

"There are many reasons, Emad," Zareen said, watching Ghada prepare the tea as a way to keep from staring at his face. At those eyes. Bright blue ocean eyes.

"Such as?"

"Thwarting evil, for one," she said, understanding how melodramatic those words sounded, even in her own ears. "What the Italians did to Jaghbub cannot be countenanced by anyone with a measure of ethics. Leveling a city and imprisoning the population is evil."

Emad nodded again, possibly not trusting himself to speak now. She could see fire in those eyes when she looked.

"It is a small matter, on the scale of things, but it lets me thumb my nose at them in a language they will understand," Zareen said. "It will aid the Senussi cause, by showing them that they have allies, even if those must remain largely secret for now. Because of this new aircraft, we have a once-in-a-life-time opportunity to do something big, because after this they will know to expect us. To watch for us. Even Italians will eventually figure something out."

He did smile now, twisted and wry as it might be. The Italians claimed to have successfully captured Abyssinia over the recent summer, but nobody had likely asked an Abyssinian their opinion on the topic.

"You asked for a short list of men we might rescue," Emad finally spoke.

Zareen nodded at him to continue as Ghada steeped the tea.

"The Emir sent three names, known to be imprisoned at Bengasi and at risk of being executed if the Italians ever organize themselves," he continued.

"I'm not sure the Italian Army could organize an orgy in a whorehouse, Emad," she replied, grinning as he grinned back. An honest smile, and not something forced in polite company.

"Just so, Zareen," he agreed. "The names I was given were Tareq al-Amin, Abdallah Zaman, and my old teacher Khaled Samara."

"Your teacher?" she asked, surprised.

Zareen would have thought anybody with that close of ties to the Cyrenaican Royal House would have already been killed as retaliation for rebellion.

"He was a Mufti, rather than a Qadi," Emad said. "A scholar of the law and the Quran, rather than a proper magistrate in a court. Those were first on the list of the invaders, when they sought to stamp out Senussi culture and history."

"Three men we could manage," Zareen said, flashing back to the interior of the new aircraft. That smoking lounge where everyone expected her to place a bomb bay at some point.

If she did that, however, she would lose the ability to haul escaped prisoners from their captivity.

She would need to speak with Hans and Finn, and

perhaps Asher and Magdy, about the ability to completely reconfigure the interior of the craft.

"So I expected, when I contacted the Emir," Emad replied. "There are probably dozens we could free, given time, but that is the one thing we lack, as all too soon your enemies will know your new capabilities. And thank you."

"For?" she asked, caught off guard.

"It was unnecessary for you to engage yourself in my war, in spite of how the others might feel on the topic," he said.

Zareen studied the man closely now, not as a potential lover, but as an ally. She had known the man for less than three weeks at this point, but he had proven himself reliable and honorable at every turn, even when he had no reason to be.

She would gamble on the man, just as she might Finn. Hans and Asher would take longer to bring around, but she had no doubt that she could, given time to wear their objections down.

"We share a second war, Emad al-Sadri," she pronounced now, watching him flinch unrelated to the tea arriving between them.

It was as though an electric spark passed between them on the arc of her words.

He stopped breathing. It was a good sign. She took that to mean he understood the seriousness of the words coming.

"You are fighting against the Italians, yes," she said. "But they were there before Mussolini. You are also warring against the colonialist mentality that sees Europeans deciding that they should determine the shape and fate of the world, just as they did in the last century in Africa."

Zareen took a cup of tea and placed it directly into his

hands, else he might not have moved, a rabbit watching a hawk overhead.

"I have a war against the colonizers, as well," Zareen finally admitted, hearing even Ghada gasp that the words might be shared with an outsider. "After we have done what we need to against the Italians, I intend to turn my mind to Persia next."

He sipped, but it was automatic, so far had he retreated inside himself.

"All of this quest for technology was not merely to help thwart the Mussolinis and Hitlers of the world, Emad," she continued. "But also the British, the Russians, and anyone else intent on keeping Persia in bondage. Do you understand me now?"

He did breathe. She heard it, slight as it was. Eyes flickered at her, at Ghada, at the tea, even at the ocean out the balcony.

"Can you?" he finally asked.

"That was why I wanted to know the secrets of The Man With No Face, Emad," she said. "He is an alien on this planet, so his technology must be so far in advance of ours that I could drive the British out. Crush the Russians and drive them back to their ancestral homelands in the far north."

"A new Persian Empire?" he probed.

"No," Zareen said. "Something even better."

"What?"

"Freedom."

CHAPTER SEVEN

Finn sat on the couch and waited for the man to work up the actual grumbles to say something. Hans was almost as predictable as the dawn. It was late in the afternoon, so sitting in a chair and drinking some scotch and soda from a bottle that came with the room was acceptable.

Even to snobby people.

"I left Germany for a reason," Hans finally announced gruffly, his own glass half-empty now.

Just enough to grind off whatever burr had kept him from talking before this.

They might have flown together for more than two years at this point. You learn a lot about a fellow, sleeping in the same crowded hotel room because the airline was too cheap to spring for individuals. Or sleeping in a hammock outside while the big Kraut was inside *Cerberus* snoring.

"Understand that, buddy," Finn replied. "Don't figure she'd come up with something this cockamamie if it wasn't for a good cause."

"Even dressing like those scum is bad," Hans continued,

voice barely above a grumble. "I am still a patriot, but I am a patriot to Germany, not to that Austrian son of a diseased camel in Berlin."

"We're going to do this to his very good buddy, Benito," Finn pointed out, unnecessarily, but firmly. Hans would get all maudlin if he didn't think you were listening to him. "And I guarantee you that it's gonna piss off a lot of those folks in Berlin, if the story ever gets out."

"If?" Hans stared at him, taking another sip.

"Fellow gets hit with something that embarrassing, does he really want to go tell everyone in the neighborhood what a screw-up he is?" Finn grinned. "Locals might not bother mentioning it to the folks in Rome. If they did, it might be to complain about what us good little Germans did to them. At which point..."

"At which point it turns into a shitshow of denial and finger-pointing, to use your favorite phrase." Hans did grin a little now. "Can we pull it off?"

"Not worried about the little lady," Finn turned serious. "Figure there's a lot better ways to lose all your money than to bet against her."

"True," the big kraut nodded.

"So what's really bothering you, Hans?" Finn pressed.

His glass had somehow sprung a leak or something, so he rose to refill it. Hans, seated on the bed, handed him another glass with its own leak.

Finn set to work refilling them, careful not to spill a drop. They were staying in a nice place, courtesy of Zareen's various contacts, so this was good scotch.

Not like the crap he used to run in and around Chicago.

Hans was lost in thought. No surprise. That was why it

was a good time to refill glasses, after all. German predictability.

"I don't want to be one of them," he finally said, taking a sip from a new round as Finn got back to his chair. "I don't like where the thought of being one of them puts my mind, Finn. *Verstehst du?*"

"Oh, I understand fine, Hans," Finn nodded, also sipping. "It would have been like me staying with Yanna and putting on a nice suit every day so I could go be a business-man. Even worse than me wearing one of those silly caps you had in Germany."

He paused to share a chuckle with his best friend.

"But who said you had to be serious?" Finn asked.

"*Was?*"

"They're Italians, the fine folk we'll be doing this to," Finn nodded. "Comical, ignorant folk. Especially if they've been assigned to a prison in a colony somewhere, instead of being in Rome with the important folks. *Ja?*"

"*Ja.*"

"So if you play the dumbest caricature of a stupid German putz, and I mean overplay it to the hilt, who are they to argue with you?" Finn grinned. "Your Uncle Fritzie, for example."

He could tell that Hans wasn't sure whether to spit on the floor or roll his eyes at Uncle Fritzie, the one who had joined the Nazi Party in 1924 and gone all in on the stupid.

The man still couldn't get promoted beyond neighbor-hood gossip, even after the Party had taken over the govern-ment and run everybody else out of town on a rail.

Stupid Uncle Fritzie, the Nazi panda bear.

"*Ja,*" Hans said with newfound wonder in his voice. His back straightened out. "Fritzie is the sort of man that someone important would send to Cyrenaica to pick up prisoners, without even bothering to send the right paperwork ahead of time. A clown show."

He took a hard drink of his scotch now and Finn could see the wheels starting to move in the man's head.

Like clockwork, in every sense of the word.

"Yes, Fritzie will play well with the abject stupidity of the sorts of people we normally meet in Bengasi, won't he?" Hans grinned.

Finn grinned back. He'd wondered, on more than one occasion, if the folks in Rome sent some of these people to the Libyan colonies just so that the Keystone Kops were out of sight.

Pretty soon he'd find out.

CHAPTER EIGHT

Asher knew doubt.

It was a novel experience for an electronic life form who had never been programmed for such a thing. At the same time, he had been sent here to learn, and given enough latitude in his programming to develop himself as needed by various situations.

Nobody had ever actually expected the mission to run this long without debriefing and updates. And it shouldn't have, except that the Durren's ship had suffered some manner of malfunction, causing it to suddenly tip over, fall from the sky, and slam into the side of a mountain at speed.

The ensuing fireball had killed all the organics and burned off his camouflage flesh, leaving him alone on this world.

Worse, the mission had been secret. An illegal sociological survey. If anyone from the Durren did come, they would arrest him, impound his datacore, and probably dismantle the frame.

Not exactly the brightest way to fail, but damnably close.

So he was stuck here. Worse, the humans had finally come to understand what he was, his own mistakes catching up at last to pinpoint his weaknesses.

At least in choosing sides, he had selected the better of the two. He hoped.

Zareen Shirazi was about to engage in activities that would push the margins of Asher's programming, even the portions he had written himself to allow certain things never envisioned by the Durren.

He could, he knew, simply walk off the beach here in Alexandria headed north into the depths of the Mediterranean Ocean and vanish forever from human cognition, but he would eventually grow bored.

Worse, that might be measured in weeks, rather than decades, so much had he enjoyed his time engaging with humans over the last two decades.

But Zareen Shirazi was likely going to kill people. And he would be called upon to help in ways he had not yet even been able to calculate.

Asher's programming precluded him from injuring humans. In the past, he had been able to scare off the occasional attempted mugging, simply because no amount of human weaponry could harm his chassis. Certainly nothing that could be hand-held at current levels of technology.

Thus had his Durren masters programmed him. And it was a wise choice on their part. He was stronger than any human by an order of magnitude, and capable of calculating at several times human speeds.

He had even learned the complicated calculus of rumor-mongering. That alone would justify his time on this planet, when he was eventually arrested and shipped home.

The Durren did not fully understand this socioeconomic system called capitalism. Were the humans any less dangerous, scholars might have spent time here exploring it, especially as humans were poised on the verge of rapid technological innovation that might yet see them in near-space in this century.

In the meantime, you needed an Autonomous Simulated Human Exploration Robot to do the chore.

Fascism was even more complicated. The practicum had diverged wildly from the theoretical writings he had consumed. But it also hewed much closer to the human classification as a dangerous species.

What would a war pitting democratic capitalism against fascist socialism look like? What would the intellectual descendants of Marx do in that instance?

Would he be called upon to participate?

Worse, fight?

Hints dropped by Finnley Severijns suggested that the man had much more recent experience in armed conflict than the Great War. And Emad al-Sadri was in the middle of such a thing.

But it would be Ghada Attar that he approached for help, Asher decided after reviewing all the files.

She was an expert in close combat, using forms that were both armed and unarmed. Asher had watched the woman practice several mornings, purely from a curiosity standpoint because it appeared to be a form of dance, except that he had also seen several of those same maneuvers sped up greatly and used to do non-permanent damage to the French assassin known simply as Bertrand.

It was the non-permanent part that appealed to him.

If Asher could render a fragile human unconscious but not permanently broken, then perhaps he could remain faithful to his original programming, rather than becoming entirely rogue.

It was a given that the Durren would dismantle him when that posse finally ran him to ground, to use a saying Finn liked. But he could at least go to his hanging with his head held high.

Who would have ever imagined?

CHAPTER NINE

"What have you learned?" Didier asked as he admitted the assassin into his new room.

He had asked the manager to change his rooms once he knew that the old one had been compromised. It would not prevent The Man With No Face from returning, but Didier could not sleep in his old bed, knowing that the Man had been there.

He kept having nightmares where he awoke to that mask floating over him. He had never seen it, but the description had been sufficient for Didier to include a drawing in his notebook.

Perhaps the Man would miss him on a return.

He was not hurting for money, even with the nearly thousand pounds that had been stolen. Merely needed to have more funds wired from his bank in Paris, at the cost of a day of his life to get everything organized.

Didier closed the door and returned to his table and the cigarette still slowly smoldering down. Bertrand took his usual spot on the bed.

"I may have a lead," he said simply.

It was everything Didier could do not to jump up, grab the man, and shake him in his barely contained frustration. Bertrand even tensed in a manner suggesting that he was aware of the risk.

"Tell me," Didier ground out.

"A contact in Port Said has contacted me," the man continued. "The aircraft known as *Cerberus*, a Ford Trimotor with Aurora Italia markings, was seen there, apparently having flown directly from Cairo."

"Port Said?" Didier asked.

Was the woman intent on traveling via ship somewhere next? Had she already give up on The Man With No Face?

No, she must have recruited him. That was the only explanation for the twinned disappearance.

"However," Bertrand continued quickly, "it appears that the aircraft has traveled now to Alexandria, if the rumors are correct. Worse, it is being sold, as my contact in Port Said telegraphed a coded message that Magdy the arms merchant is involved, possibly purchasing the craft."

"Indeed?" Didier said. "But they are not in Port Said now?"

"*Cerberus* is not," Bertrand confirmed. "I am concerned that they may have sold the plane and vanished."

"Understood," Didier said, crushing out the last of his cigarette and rising to pace. "All leads in Cairo have gone cold. These are thin threads, but all we have at present. Do we know where this Magdy person is?"

"He has not been seen in Cairo in several days at this point, but we are at a remove, learning the secrets of the other two cities," the lean assassin replied.

"Yes," Didier acknowledged. "We must chase the woman

again, as before. But this time she has assistants beyond that Persian maid, so we must locate them first, it seems."

He pivoted on his foot and studied the killer.

"We shall leave for Alexandria first thing in the morning, Bertrand," he decided. "Go pack immediately and I will contact the hotel manager to forward everything. Find us a car or something to Alexandria, so that we can be there after lunch. I have a feeling that we must pounce on her, else she might slip away again and this time we will have a much harder game to track her."

"Why is that?"

"If she is selling the aircraft, she might buy a new one," Didier replied. "One we do not know yet. As she has her own pilot on staff, she would not be limited by the number of commercial carriers or ships departing Egypt, and thus we might lose her until someone is willing to contact us wherever she arrives. What mischief could that woman get up to in that time?"

The assassin nodded and rose, heading towards the door without another word.

Alone, Didier considered his duels with the woman over the last few years. The various missions to libraries for old books. Interviews with reputed eyewitnesses. Expeditions planned but never undertaken, to places like Tunguska or others, seeking proof.

Why had she broken pattern now? Suddenly the woman had accumulated an entire team of experts, where she had been content alone before.

Unless The Man With No Face was more than he seemed.

The rumors had suggested a connection to the Gabal El Uweinat. She had gone there, and immediately after her return had fled from Didier, working to maintain her invisibility. And mentioned parts of a crashed alien spaceship she had supposedly found, but Didier knew Shirazi to be a consummate liar when she needed to be.

At the same time, he was willing to admit that he and Bertrand had perhaps scared off the man in their clumsiness, but all traces had disappeared, when normally someone might only hide for a few days, or a week at most.

The Man With No Face had been gone for four weeks now.

Had he fled Egypt?

Was Zareen Shirazi pursuing him even now and had a lead?

All the more reason to catch her before she could leave Egypt.

What if The Man With No Face really was an alien in disguise?

CHAPTER TEN

Finn studied the results with a jaundiced eye.

"What do you think, my friend?" Magdy the arms merchant, standing right next to him in the hangar, asked with an oily tone.

Friendly and all, but it still left you understanding that the man was a criminal.

Worse than Finn had been.

Okay, maybe just as bad. Asher had a high opinion of the fellow, and Finn had come to like Asher.

And he had to admit that the results were astonishing.

He walked closer, aware that everyone else was trailing behind him.

The Heinkel 111-K was an impressive craft. Twice as fast as *Cerberus.* Twice the range. Way more cargo space.

Modern.

He just didn't like the need to paint it that Nazi gray, or put that big, damned swastika on the tail. Weren't keeping either one a second longer than immediately necessary.

He turned to Magdy and nodded.

"Looks good enough to piss on," Finn observed with a grim smile.

That was what the man really wanted. Appreciation that his criminal contacts had taken the plane and made it look like a civilian transport for the Nazi Party. The kind that might land someplace and disgorge a small team of supposed *Übermenshen* to talk down to the local Italian cops and soldiers.

Showing them how it was supposed to be done, as it were.

Finn turned to Hans, sharing that man's grimace.

"Ja," Hans said. "*Gut* enough to piss on."

Finn nodded to Zareen and Asher. It was their show now.

Asher surprised him by pulling an envelope from a pocket and handing it to Magdy. The Egyptian opened it and began to thumb notes.

"I included a bonus for speed," Asher said. "Our mission will require that we strike rapidly. Afterwards, I hope you can remove that unsightly stain for something more friendly. And less likely to get us shot down somewhere."

"As you have instructed, Asher," Magdy said with his own grin. "So shall it be. I thank all of you for the business and will depart now so that none may accuse me later of any level of complicity beyond the mercantile."

Finn chuckled along with the others as the man returned to the car that had brought them to this hangar on the desert-side edge of Alexandria. Finn, Hans, and Emad joined him long enough to grab the various trunks and boxes they had brought along today, with most of their gear either already aboard, or safe in storage at the hotel under Emad's name.

That ought to throw off a bunch of folks, especially if they were looking for Zareen.

Or Italian creditors who wanted to ask about an airplane that had apparently vanished.

Whoops.

Zareen had a strange look on her face as he got close, so Finn stopped right in front of the woman and set the trunk down.

"It'll work," he said.

Her face said otherwise.

They'd all gone over the plan a dozen times. Emad had grown up on the Libyan coast, mostly farther east, but he had traveled quite a bit as a kid. Finn and Hans had used Bengasi as a transit point between Tripoli and Tobruk, on their regular runs down from Rome to points beyond Cairo.

And both he and Emad had previously carried guns for a living.

"I have my doubts," she said quietly enough that maybe only Ghada heard besides him, the other three guys currently stashing things in the back of the stolen condor.

"They're Italians, Zareen," Finn tried to reassure her.

He'd had a lot of experience with Italians, most of it bad when you got to the official levels. Oh sure, they were pretty good at sealing off the border against Senussi rebels by building a wire fence two hundred and seventy kilometers long. And had bombed the Abyssinians back to the stone age, or something like that. But just his time at the Bengasi airport had left Finn's respect for those folks lacking.

Must have left it in his other suit.

"Hey, worse comes to worst, we can always come back and bomb them with Nazi colors," Finn grinned. "That ought to be all sorts of fun, especially if we time it just right to come at sunset. Big, lumbering German aircraft appears and is spotted. Then it drops bombs, blows things up, and turns back out to sea, running faster than those stupid biplanes the Italians are using these days."

"The mission is supposed to be quiet, Finn," she said. "Slip in, confuse them, slip back out with prisoners being shipped off to Berlin because we've discovered that they are even more dangerous than the folks in Rome imagine."

"You work it like that, and I'll be happy," Finn said. "But we're also prepared for alternative contingencies."

"That's why I hired you," she nodded, turning to the others, all watching carefully from over there and not coming over here to chat. "Shall we?"

"After you, mistress," Finn said, picking up his box.

She was in charge. He was just the hired help, with a pretty good view of that bottom—both bottoms—as Ghada was dressed in more western clothing today, rather than her usual desert robes.

It was all going to be a huge vaudeville act when they got there.

This one just happened to have guns.

CHAPTER ELEVEN

Zareen knew herself to be possessed by unnecessary doubts, but it could not be helped. None of what she was doing had official imprimatur, from any of the governments or organizations that helped fund her various adventures and missions under one form or another over the last several years.

A few of them might be rather put out if they discovered the deepest levels of her plans, but that could not be helped. She was British, and willing to use that half of her soul ruthlessly to help the Persian half.

The Italians and Germans might make silly noises about liberating the world from colonial oppression, but she had her expectations.

There was liberation, and then there was *liberation*.

Only one of those saw Persia retake its place among the first states of the world. The other would replace English overlords and advisors for German ones.

The plane rumbled out of the hangar and the noise fell off. Shortly, they would head out into the desert on a south-westerly heading, gaining elevation until they were out of sight from the ground. Then, a long loop around north, crossing out to sea. Finally headed way out over the water until they turned back and approached Bengasi from the northeast, as though coming down from Rome on a direct flight.

Or as direct as possible. Finn would have all those details, if anyone asked. Hans was just helping him fly until they could land and the man would turn into a high-level Party official, only a step below her. And two steps above Emad.

Only Ghada didn't really have a role to play here. Or rather, she would continue to play her role as innocent maid to an important person. While prepared at any moment to kill someone.

Asher was not with them, remaining in Alexandria for a time, as it was too dangerous for someone who could not pass as human.

And if everything went wrong, he would at least be safe.

Thus, she had her doubts.

The plane leapt into the air with a furious roar and climbed. She was aft in the smoking compartment with Emad and Ghada.

"You look concerned," Emad offered, trying to look friendly without prying.

"This probably rates in the top five dumbest things I have ever attempted," Zareen replied.

"Only top five?" he asked, perhaps a little more shocked than he should be. "Not number one?"

She supposed he still saw her as an English noblewoman. Or a Persian princess. Not a rugged adventurer capable of feats on her own, daring without some man to share his glory with her.

"Sneaking into the Soviet Union to explore the rumors

about Tunguska was probably the most dangerous," she said. "They are rather fickle about foreigners, and have a tendency to just imprison people into camps rather than sort them out or throw them out of the country."

She turned to share a secret grin with Ghada before speaking again.

"Guatemala and the Yucatan were also extremely dangerous, because there were active wars going on, as well as poisonous snakes everywhere you walked," she continued. "This is just a caper into an Italian city, with bluff, bluster, and guns."

"I see," he said, probably not seeing. He gestured at the trunks stashed farther back. "And all that will not help?"

"It only takes one person deciding to arrest us and then call someone to unmask it all, Emad," she said, sobering. "Then we can all be executed as spies, if they chose. We dance on a delicate ledge."

"Indeed," he agreed. "But each time I lead my men out into the desert to raid an Italian or French target, we all had an expectation that death might be our pay. It is the nature of the business."

Zareen suppressed her flinch at the mention of the French. Chad had not been that far away when she met the man, and a number of native empires of the interior had been erased or were slowly being ground out of existence by the French, even as the Italians and English were doing the same in their own, respective corners.

It made sense that the Senussi would not limit themselves to just one colonial opponent, even as others helped for their own, jealous reasons. British Egypt would not host the Grand Senussi if they did not harbor expectations that he could rile up Italian Cyrenaica at some future need.

Pawns and Bishops, moving as they could around the board, but available to be sacrificed later.

"I still have one concern," Emad continued when she did not reply. "Neither you nor I can pass as proper Nazis, at least as far as I understand their propaganda about being the master race. How will we fool the Italians?"

"Partly, that is why I needed Hans," she said. "He will fool them. And your blue eyes will mark you as European, regardless of your skin. One of my nannies growing up was German, and I speak with a Hamburg accent. Plus I can speak fluent Italian, so I will do most of the talking."

"Are there any languages you don't speak?" he asked, astonished.

Zareen considered it. English, Farsi, German, Italian, French, Arabic. Enough Russian to travel but not impersonate a local. Similarly enough Mandarin, Cantonese, and Japanese to get by.

"Most of the Indian subcontinent eludes me," she finally admitted. "Central America was interesting, because it seemed that every valley had a different dialect related to the pre-Columbian tongues rather than Spanish. But I passed myself off as French there and that met with their approval."

She watched the man's pupils dilate. Shock, she supposed. Even an educated Senussi nobleman like Emad al-Sadri spoke Arabic and Italian. Emad was pretty good in English, but that was himself, rather than his culture. Similarly, probably a little French.

However, he had never, as far as she knew, traveled beyond Egypt, Sudan, Chad, and his native Cyrenaica.

If he stayed with her, the man was likely to see the entire planet eventually. The Man With No Face was just a small facet of her overall plans.

Emad lapsed into quiet. She did the same.

After a time, the newly installed intercom came to life.

"Hey, folks," Finn announced. "We've leveled off and are now cruising. Feel free to move about and start getting dressed. Hans will be back shortly as well, and then we'll swap when he's ugly. Well, uglier."

Zareen heard something muttered by the German, but it did not come through. Just the laughter.

That was good.

Where she was going, she would need to carry with her a little laughter.

Because the next Great War was just about to begin.

CHAPTER TWELVE

Asher had changed his mask at the same time he had changed his robes.

He dressed these days more like a successful merchant than one of the poorest of the poor. Nobody in Alexandria knew him, so he needed to blend in better with people, lest the authorities decide to take exception to his presence someday and arrest him.

Attempt to arrest him.

He could easily outrun any human. And on the crowded streets of Alexandria, most motor vehicles.

The Mediterranean was always an option, if all else failed. He could be in Lebanon in a week or so if needed.

Today, he had a corner table to himself and an arrangement with the owner, much as he had kept with Faisal for so long, upriver in Cairo. Rent, such as it was, paid in cash each morning to offset the traffic that might be lost as a result of someone at a table all day not drinking tea.

Robots could not. The Man With No Face simply

departed for a brief period occasionally as though biological demands needed to be met.

Eventually, he would become a fixture here, if he stayed in this city as long as he had Cairo.

Philosophical ruminations led him nowhere, but that was acceptable. People needed to know where to find him.

The right people, anyway.

Mustafa entered, glancing around the semi-gloom before moving toward Asher with purpose.

Asher nodded to the owner and the man appeared with tea beginning to steep.

Mustafa sat first, but was not surprised when tea arrived unrequested. He simply placed a coin on the table and Asher prepared to extend his ongoing explorations of human culture and capitalism.

The owner departed and Asher studied his guest.

"There is news?" he asked unnecessarily.

Mustafa was another one like Magdy, although he was more of a simple smuggler and less an illicit arms dealer.

Still, Asher had been able to make arrangements with a number of friends of friends in Alexandria.

"There is," Mustafa nodded, glancing around once more in the most guilty manner Asher could imagine before returning to Asher's new mask. "Didier Beauchêne and his assassin arrived in town a few hours ago and have already begun hunting for you and the woman Shirazi."

"Do they have any leads as yet?" Asher asked, thankful that the woman and her crew of killers had already departed on their mission.

He was also apprehensive that they might return to Alexandria successful and blunder into the two Frenchmen, neither of whom were likely to respond well, as badly embarrassed as they had been by Finn and Emad rescuing the women from probable torture.

Things were likely to get out of hand, and he was still bound by his programming not to injure humans.

"They have no leads," Mustafa replied. "But they are willing to offer larger bribes than normal, as they have not yet taken the time to build up a network of friends, such as you have done. It is only a matter of time before some songbird whispers in their ears. Magdy might have returned to Cairo, perhaps passing the Frenchmen on the road as he did, but many of Magdy's people here are likely to talk, even amongst themselves."

"Such is human nature, Mustafa," Asher said. "I believe it behooves us to create an even larger distraction. Can you make arrangements for someone to fly me to Port Said this afternoon? And then spread that rumor on the streets? That will draw the Frenchman in my wake and away from my friends."

"You have never had friends, Asher," the Egyptian man said, a jolt of surprise running through him. "Only contacts and dealers in rumor and material. Even you have said as much, as long as I have known you."

"The world has changed, Mustafa," Asher said, carefully parsing his syntax to obscure as much as he revealed.

Mustafa would sell on his information to others. That was the nature of the business and their relationship. Useful tidbits got traded like goods, facilitating communications back and forth in a vast web that connected all humans eventually.

And one Durren robot hiding amongst them.

"Changed?" the man asked, perking up.

"Italy is not satisfied with their Libyan colonies, nor with

Abyssinia," Asher explained. "They have their eyes on Egypt as well. The Senussi resist. The Egyptians would like to be free, but neither the British nor the Italians will allow it. However, at present we are better served by the British, for reasons that should not be discussed in a tea house."

Asher cringed, but those words would get repeated a dozen times once Mustafa left. Perhaps a thousand people would take up a new rallying cry, turning the Egyptians away from any possible liberation by the Italians. But Asher had heard about Cyrenaica from a native. And the reports coming out of Abyssinia were not promising.

Italy was slowly working its way up to attacking Egypt as well. Perhaps as the opening act to the coming Great War. Maybe only as a localized thing that might not get as out of hand as the last one had.

"You have chosen sides, my friend?" Mustafa asked, disbelief evident in his voice.

"I have," Asher said carefully, listening for any of his internal circuits to overheat or melt as he pressed so hard against the edge of his programming.

However, the British at least stood for fair play, even as they fell short of their own ideals time and again. The Americans would likely ally with the English again. They had a dream that even the Durren could come away impressed by.

"One of my new allies is Senussi," Asher continued, allowing Mustafa to know that much.

Jaghbub had been an Egyptian city, as recently as twelve years ago, before the two countries shifted their borders around and the Senussi heartland was suddenly subject to Italian law.

And to Italian atrocities, as the city was later simply

destroyed and the population carted off to concentration camps to make space for colonizing farmers to step in instead.

"Senussi?" Mustafa recoiled slightly at the revelation.

There were a number of such refugees on this side of the border now. That fence had been erected to keep them out.

It had mostly worked.

And now the locals would understand that The Man With No Face had chosen sides, when so many of his compatriots were agnostic in their dealings. Not amoral, usually. Never unethical.

Still, willing to deal with anyone having needs, whether criminal, citizen, or government official.

Asher had drawn a line in the sand.

Word would get out.

"Senussi," Asher confirmed firmly. "The flight to Port Said, as noisy as it must be on my part, is to draw my enemies away from my allies, as I cannot contact them at present to warn them that our common foe has found us again and that they are at risk."

Our common foe? Indeed.

A robot sociologist had analyzed the available information and decided that he could intervene in human affairs.

Not enough to utterly derail their development, unless he failed, but he could help.

Asher wasn't an engineer, capable of telling Zareen how to make superweapons, but he supposed that just by studying him or the wreckage out there in the desert, she would be able to make technological advancements that help the British.

At least until she threw them over for her true love.

Humans did not generally understand the sensitivity of his ears to listen to someone's heart rate as they spoke.

Zareen Shirazi was assisting the British for the same reasons Asher was. They were the better of the two choices today.

That would change tomorrow, but he needed to reach tomorrow intact in order to watch it unfold.

Asher rose abruptly, surprising Mustafa. He drew his own coin from a pocket and left it next to the first.

"Come," he ordered his other ally. "We need to make a very noisy getaway at the airport and then move my flight outward from Port Said. I will need your help, Mustafa."

The Egyptian man studied him for a long moment before rising as well.

"Has the war begun, Asher?" he asked, falling into stride as they made their way to the door.

"Mine has," Asher replied gravely.

Behind them, the tea had not even steeped.

CHAPTER THIRTEEN

Finn hated the outfit, snazzy as it might look. Civilian, but with military aspirations and influences, so soldiers would automatically snap to.

Russet tunic jacket with a brown Sam Browne belt. White shirt. Black tie. Black slacks. Black shoes. He even had a cute saucer hat to wear, right up to the point that he put it all in a barrel with some gasoline and let those folks know what he really thought of them.

Hans was dressed better, in a gray that he and Zareen shared. Probably made them look like senior people or something.

Finn was just the pilot on this caper. Land the plane. Supervise any mechanics he could swindle into refueling it. Wait for Zareen to return with her packages and fly them all out to sea to disappear.

Happy making.

In the near distance, Bengasi was visible, fading into that weird dusky sunset you got around here, where things faded slowly through the reds before the day finally ended.

He'd be on the ground in about twenty minutes. Late in an Italian's day, when they wanted to just go have a bottle of wine and some pasta, rather than dealing with a plane full of just-arrived Nazi officials with attitude problems.

Worse come to worst, he could always make it someplace friendly with the fuel on board, but Finn was hoping everything went smoothly.

Hell, he'd even hidden his Colt for a Walther pistol that had come with the uniform. Talk about commitment to a role.

"All hands, we are in descent into Bengasi," Finn announced over the intercom with a cheerful lilt. "The rest of you will be on in a few minutes."

Finn smiled and flew this as though he'd gotten desperate enough to take that job with Luft Hansa, back before he ended up in Rome instead.

They might have even made him wear something like this all the time, if that had happened. At least until things got ugly enough that he had to skip town.

Again.

Finn had gotten to be pretty good at that, over the years.

In the distance, the runway he normally landed on waited invitingly for him to touch down.

Hopefully, nobody on the ground recognized him, but he'd shaved while in flight, and was even wearing a pressed shirt AND a tie.

Nobody here but us good, little Germans. You'll believe that, right?

CHAPTER FOURTEEN

Unlike her fellows, Zareen was used to costume balls where she arrived pretending to be someone she was not. That sort of behavior frequently described her life as a spy anyway, if you wished to be niggling and technical.

Today, the black and gray of a senior Nazi party official. Jodhpurs, because she did jodhpurs. Made men look at her legs and bottom instead of her face. Useful if you didn't want them necessarily remembering your visage later. Gray tunic cut and belted to emphasize her hips and barely there bosom for the same reasons. Hair up in a tight braid. Just enough makeup to accentuate and distract. Shirt crisp. Tie tight.

She nodded to Emad as Hans came aft and the Senussi man opened the hatch, deploying the steps down.

A German bomber arriving off schedule should be a big enough deal that even the Italians would take notice and send a car around.

If not, she would send Emad to walk the distance, with instructions to be unpleasant when he arrived.

There were roles to be fulfilled here.

It appeared that someone had panicked, based on the speed with which a staff car was even now roaring recklessly across the airport.

Zareen had a flashback to the big Mercedes that had taken her to first meet Finn so that she might hire the man.

Had it hardly been two weeks ago?

This was not a Mercedes, but looked safe enough. She took up her position to Hans's right and came to something vaguely military in her posture. Hans had fallen in on himself, but his only job was to glower menacingly at people while she did the fast talking. Emad and Ghada were along to provide mass, but not entertainment.

Everyone here spoke German, but not everyone understood how to bluff minor functionaries and low-ranking officers. That was her job.

The car approached at a mad sprint, but came to a more sedate rest. She didn't think that Emad had actually threatened them with his submachine gun, but he had rested a hand on it.

Then again, the man knew how to effectively convey things non-verbally.

The car stopped and a driver sprang out, racing around to open a rear door for another man still tying a tie as he stepped into the sun. Luck had the fool facing west, so he was also probably blinded.

Zareen strode forward crisply and addressed the newcomer. The stranger was tall and lean in a manner similar to Hans, but not as *anything* as the bigger German.

Weak and soft. But then, he was an airport official in a minor portion of an Italian colony.

"Have the orders arrived?" Zareen began her conversation in the middle as the man reacted to her. Her Italian was frosted over with a German accent.

"Orders?" the man almost shrank in on himself.

The driver smartly raced back to his place to escape whatever was going to happen next.

"Orders, Lieutenant," she snapped. "Herr Donnar is here to collect our prisoners and return them to Berlin. Have they been prepared for transit?"

Just for extra impact, she pulled out an envelope that had been stolen at some point from a Nazi courier. Waved it under the man's nose, it was like a red cape in front of a bull. Except it had the exact opposite effect.

The Italian went utterly pale under that swarthy skin.

"No, signorina," he stammered painfully. "Nobody has informed me of anything. I came because no aircraft were expected today. Especially not a German one."

"Where is your superior officer?" she growled up at the man, taking another step forward in apparent anger.

He actually staggered a step backwards.

"He is not available, signorina," the officer quailed. "And left strict orders not to be disturbed."

Zareen let her eyes get narrow and cruel.

"Off with his mistress?" she menaced him with her words like a knife. "Perhaps gone on holiday with a whole bevy of them or something?"

The man snapped hard to attention, eyes on some distant horizon, rather than reply.

Bingo.

Zareen turned to Hans with exasperation.

"Herr Donnar, they seem ill-prepared to offer us proper hospitality," she announced in German, using a loud enough voice that everyone understood her.

"Indeed?" Hans growled angrily, walking like a hungry blond bear as he got close.

Hans had height, breadth, and mass on the nervous Italian, who actually gulped audibly.

"Are you important enough to see to my issues, boy?" Hans asked in a voice like a razor blade. "Or should I see who else has failed me today and destroy them?"

It was like someone else was there when she glanced at the big German. Gone was the affable mechanic who knew several dirty jokes that didn't translate out of German all that well.

This was someone's idealized Nazi bastard.

Zareen already hated the fellow, whoever he was.

"I will take care of it, sir," the man stammered.

Zareen was almost surprised that the fool didn't piss himself right now, from the tone of his voice.

"See that you do," Hans continued in that hard, lethal voice. "You will take me to the place where my prisoners are being held. Now."

Give the man credit, he actually settled his shoulders and turned to her to speak, rather than risk the big man's wrath.

"Which prisoners should have been transferred?" he asked nervously.

Zareen made a production out of opening the courier pouch and withdrawing a paper without any letterhead, unfolding it and studying the names for a long moment before speaking.

"Tareq al-Amin," she began. "Khaled Samara. Abdalla Zaman. These men have been identified as threats to the Reich and need to be taken directly to Berlin for interrogation by *my experts*."

Zareen wrapped her tongue lovingly around those words,

portraying herself as the sort of woman who kept professional torturers on staff. She even smiled at the Italian and licked her lips, just so he had no doubts as to the fate of those men when they did get to Berlin.

Fellow went completely white. It was almost like someone had flipped off a light switch, and then flipped it back on a moment later.

"Immediately, sir," he snapped his heels in the German manner. Probably the first time in his life he had ever done so.

Turning on his heel, he gestured Herr Donnar and Fraulein Schmidt into the vehicle.

Hans went first, followed by Ghada and Emad. Zareen smiled at the man and pointed to the front door.

"Herr Donnar is tired from the long trip and likely to be snappish," she said in a quiet, conspiratorial tone better engaged in romantic romps than assassinations, just to further whipsaw the man. "You ride up front and get us to the place where the prisoners are. I will make sure he does not hold you personally accountable for the failures of your commander."

Again, that lick of the lips, like she was the sort of woman who grew aroused at the thought of blood and pain.

Inflicting it.

Zareen had actually known such a woman. A French aristocrat who spent most of her time in Edinburgh preying upon the locals. And being preyed upon as well.

Praying mantis best described her, so she made a lovely model for this role.

The Italian threw himself into the front seat like it was a lifeboat. Zareen took her place in back next to Hans.

"He will see to your needs, Herr Donnar," she said

primly, aware that someone up front might be able to over-hear them, even with the panel closed.

Hit fast. Hit hard. Hit *mean*, and hope that your foe cannot recover quickly enough to stop you.

It had gotten her into and out of Lisbon.

Hopefully, it would see her through Bengasi.

CHAPTER FIFTEEN

Mein Gott, but Hans hated Uncle Fritzie. Fortunately, the man had come from the Mendelsohn side of the family, Hans's mother, so he didn't have the size or mass of the Fertig boys.

Hans could see where that might have made him into the sort of man that the Nazis back home would have promoted beyond neighborhood snoop and gossip. But he doubted anybody actually *liked* Fritz Mendelsohn.

Still, it was a part that Hans could play. Glowering with barely-leashed rage. On Fritzie, it frequently came across as being threatened by a Pomeranian princess of a hound, if something that small could maul you.

Hans didn't like it. Didn't like himself doing it. Wouldn't, but the *fraulein* needed him to scare poor Italians into giving her what she wanted.

Most men would do anything a woman that beautiful asked, but you had to assume the Italians would want to try to seduce her first. And last. And several times along the way.

Giacomo Casanova was not a German archetype, after all.

Hans drew a breath and stepped back into the role he hated. But that hatred would make it all the more lifelike.

He turned to the Fraulein.

"Are we confident that they will be able to deliver our charges quickly?" he asked in a loud enough tone that the men up front might hear through the panel. Or there might be a listening device so no fat, Italian commander had to yell. "I would not like to spend a night here, if we can get back as far as Rome by morning."

"The Lieutenant is taking us directly to the jail, Herr Donnar," Zareen replied, also in character with eavesdroppers around. "I will impress upon them your interest in promptness when we arrive."

"See that you do," he snarled the words, thinking about men Fritzie had threatened in bars over the years.

Fritzie Mendelsohn was only dangerous because he had the power to denounce someone. To have strangers arrive in the dead of night with guns and make someone disappear.

Beating the man would not have changed Fritzie's behavior. Not unless Hans made sure it was a permanent condition of dead.

The thought had crossed his mind, but it was too late now.

Should have beaten all the Nazi's to death, instead of letting them take over Germany and begin making predatory noises on everyone else. Just put all the Fritzies of the world down instead of letting them grow up to be bullies.

Hans growled to himself at where his own cowardice had landed him. Weimar had failed. Everything had failed. Twenty years after his war had ended, and all Hans had to show for it was a stolen, German aircraft, a fake uniform, and a mission to make Italians look like even bigger fools than normal.

And his friends.

The *fraulein* was counting on him. Finn and Emad as well.

He could do this.

One of these days, though, he would have an accounting with that bastard *Fritzie*.

CHAPTER SIXTEEN

It felt alien, but Emad supposed that his future in the company of Zareen would be like that. At least as long as he decided to stay near the woman.

Or until she grew tired of him and sent him back to the desert.

He watched her now out of the corner of his eye as the car exited the airfield and got out onto afternoon streets.

Emad supposed that he could call himself smitten. She was nothing at all like most of the women he had ever known. It wasn't the intellect or the class. He knew many women at least as educated as Zareen, and far wealthier.

What Zareen had was freedom. She could come and go as she chose. That was utterly unique in Emad's experience. Hell, an amazingly small number of men he knew could say such a thing, upon reflection.

Zareen Shirazi was free.

Not even Emad al-Sadri could claim that. He had been raised in a palace, however remote from the centers of power and largely ignored. But he supposed even that had worked in his favor, letting him spend time around the warriors and mechanics, rather than the perfumed courtiers.

It had let him learn to fight.

He was still fighting. Still opposing the Italians, but in a different manner.

It was just a little complicated to try to explain, even to himself, let alone to cousin Idris.

Zareen had hired Finn and Hans as permanent staff. Emad had kind of joined up at the same time, although they hadn't really addressed things.

Zareen had that power about her. That charisma.

The thing that drew you into her orbit and tucked you there. Emad hadn't pressed beyond those bounds.

Finn and Hans had made it clear that they would not interrupt, as long as he minded his manners. He had.

But nothing had happened. Partly, they had not stopped running from the Frenchman and his allies for weeks, always moving and hiding while Zareen planned her next steps. He had the impression that she might have left Egypt entirely, especially as The Man With No Face had also chosen to join her.

Zareen could have been in Lisbon by now. Emad wasn't sure why she hadn't left, except that Emad wasn't sure he could leave to follow her. To join her. Cousin Idris's letter had some latitude of ambiguity on the topic, under the rubric of *helping the resistance in other ways.*

Whatever that meant.

Would he leave? Could he?

Zareen caught him looking now and a smile flashed across her face, gone in the blink of an eye.

He could leave. He would not. He would follow this

woman to the ends of the Earth for the chance to see that smile again.

Perhaps they needed to have a conversation, just the two of them with Ghada primly chaperoning. Talk about what their future might look like.

She was not a woman to take orders from a man. Any man. She would barely give cousin Idris the courtesy of a reply, because she really was royalty, on both sides if you studied enough family trees.

The Senussi were a movement, not a family. A drive to make the world a better place by finding that middle ground between the dancers and the lawyers, where men and women could live upright, sober lives and contribute to society, but still find their own way to Allah the All-Merciful and his Prophet, *Peace Be Upon Him*.

Emad shook off such things. Those were problems for tomorrow.

Right now, the sun was getting close to setting on an Italian colony wrested with bloody hands from his family and friends.

He could not kill them all today.

But this was a beginning.

CHAPTER SEVENTEEN

Late afternoon.

Zareen watched various folks headed home from whatever they had been doing with their lives as dinner time approached. People would be tired from the long day. Distracted. Willing to generally go along, so they didn't have to work any harder right now.

She might have done something like this before.

Usually against librarians who would be willing to just answer a question to get you to stop asking more, so that they could go get their coffee or tea. Or close up for the day, if you only had the one question.

Here, the stakes would be higher. Zareen could see the need to possibly steal a truck or something, if anything went wrong. Perhaps make prisoners of the two men up front right now, depending.

However, she believed she had them reasonably well-bluffed at this point. The man had not even asked to see the papers, the so-called orders she was carrying. It was entirely possible the man didn't actually read German, but she would have doubted it.

They did look official enough for this. If someone decided to hold things up and send telegrams to Rome or Berlin, she'd be in trouble immediately anyway.

A hand tapped on the panel separating the two compartments. It opened a moment later.

"Signorina, we arrive shortly," the Lieutenant said, carefully addressing her and not the ferocious *Herr Donnar* next to her like an Olympian God of Ugly Retributions.

"Very good," Zareen said. "Have the car wait while you accompany us into the building to sort out whatever it was that went wrong with the communications."

"Understood, signorina," he said, pulling the panel shut again.

The car turned off of the main street they had been following down a narrower one, cobbled with old stones from the way the tires rattled.

The entire block on her side of the car was a wall of dressed stone at least twenty feet tall. It felt like an old prison, just looking at it.

They have a smell to them.

Midway down, a gate opened like a mouth into hell. The driver turned smartly in, passing through an outer gate and coming to a halt inside a hallway wide enough and tall enough for two trucks.

Zareen leaned forward and pulled the panel open again so she could listen.

"What is this?" a gruff, annoyed voice asked from outside the car.

"Let us in," the Lieutenant called across the vehicle. "We

have German officials with orders to pick up several prisoners and take them to Berlin."

"Germans?"

"That's right," Zareen's guide replied. "Now snap to, damn it. We are in a hurry here."

She nodded crisply.

That response sounded much more like how she expected an Italian officer to talk, however minor and irrelevant a functionary, when confronting *mere soldiers*.

It worked. The man stepped back and called something to someone else. A moment later she heard the screech of gates opening on rusty hinges, and the driver slipped the car into gear and lurched forward.

They entered a courtyard large enough for a company of men to be drawn up. Or several trucks delivering prisoners or food.

The car turned on three points and was faced outwards again when the driver and the Lieutenant both hopped out and opened doors on their sides.

Ghada and Emad emerged first.

Zareen followed a moment later, pausing to take in the scent.

That smell. Yes, it smelled like an old prison, that aroma of hopelessness that worked its way into the stone with the sweat and blood of the men held here.

She noted a half-dozen guards around her on a backless stone platform behind parapets, so this had once been someone's palace, set to defend against mobs or foreign armies. Modern firearms had long-since rendered such fortifications irrelevant, so the architecture had been adapted to the modern needs of holding prisoners.

Lights weren't on yet, but would be soon, as the shadows

were stretching enough to cast about half of this courtyard into semi-darkness. Besides this car, there was a single truck, flat-bed style with a canvas top on the back. Possibly a Ford. Possibly an Italian knockoff. Currently irrelevant to her plans, but Zareen never took anything for granted.

A man had emerged from the main building when the vehicle came to a stop. He waited for them now at the top of a short flight of stone steps.

Hans emerged finally from the rear of the vehicle, standing up and casting a spell over the entire space in a way Zareen really hadn't believed the man capable of producing.

She would need to drag him away from the aircraft more frequently, if he could channel such an effect on demand. Or she would need to find a way to impersonate more Nazi officers in the future.

Who knew what the war would bring when it came?

The Lieutenant had ascended the steps and was conferring quietly with the official. Zareen waited for Hans to approach and then led him and the other two up the steps.

Hans sighed like Atlas growing weary of his load and angry at Zeus for making him sustain it.

"Are you in charge?" he asked the man in a voice like a rusty ice saw cutting blocks.

Both Italians flinched under that tone.

"No, Herr Donnar," the prison official said nervously with a quick bow. "Signore Donati is the warden. I will conduct you to him."

At some point, Hans had pulled out a pair of black, leather gloves that Dobie had included with the costume. He held them in one hand and angrily slapped them against his other palm now. In the quiet, it sounded almost like a gunshot, echoing off the stone walls.

The local jumped. The Lieutenant flinched. Zareen realized that she didn't know either of the men's names, but a cruel, superior Nazi like her would not concern herself with mere names.

These men were only victims to be exploited. She frosted that terrible smile onto her lips and followed them, listening to the heavy thump of boots behind her as Hans followed.

Inside, the building was largely empty. Again, late afternoon, at a point where most of the office staff had probably gone home for the day. Especially as nobody had cabled ahead with notice of a special envoy arriving all the way from Berlin.

In and through, she noted a pair of Italian guards equipped with submachine guns and bored faces, presumably present to keep the prisoners from misbehaving. Neither of the boys looked dangerous. Just a pair of children taken from the farm and put into ill-fitting uniforms for a game of dress-up.

Through an office space and down a hall, the first man opened a door and stepped through. The second followed.

Zareen found herself in a larger office, one with a view of the courtyard out a pair of open windows.

A man sat behind a desk. Short, fat, bald, swarthy. If she weren't in an Italian prison, Zareen might have mistaken him for a Lebanese businessman.

Her two escorts moved around to the left side of the desk, so Zareen gestured Hans into the chair closer to them. He could keep both men at bay physically, long enough for her to draw and start shooting, if necessary.

None of the men in here looked particularly dangerous.

Ghada and Emad had not followed them in. Emad closed

the door now, presumably taking up a position to guard them against farm boys getting curious.

Hans sat. Even Zareen flinched a little when he slapped his leather gloves against his thigh and slowly scowled across the men like a turret locking on targets. They seemed on the verge of a mild panic.

Hans let go a sigh that sounded like steam escaping an angry dragon's maw more than anything, and then turned to her.

"Fraulein Schmidt, perhaps it would be best if you explained at this juncture," Hans announced in crisp, accentless German, before turning back to the Warden. A Signore Donati. "Lest my anger get out of control."

She had paid an Egyptian forger higher than going rates for the papers she pulled out now. They were quite impressive as a result, so Zareen simply extracted the envelope from the interior pocket of her jacket. Opening it, she slid out a small bundle of papers and rested them on the near side of the desk, but made no effort to hand them to anyone.

"Signore Donnar has been sent from Berlin to retrieve a set of prisoners secretly," Zareen began in Italian. "It appears that someone misunderstood the orders, or the level of secrecy involved, and so no diplomatic cable was forwarded, either to the airstrip, or here, indicating that we would be arriving today."

She left it dangling like that, patiently explaining it to the men in a tone that suggested mistakes had been made *by others,* and that perhaps these men were *not to be cashiered* in disgrace and possibly *handed over to the Nazis* for punishment as a result.

If Herr Donnar could somehow be assuaged.

There were days Zareen wondered if she could have moved to Hollywood and been successful.

Signore Donati nodded in a guarded way. The other two men were less circumspect.

With only vaguely military uniforms, German visitors might mean *Schutzstaffel*. Or worse: *Gestapo*.

Dangerous, evil men and women. The kind with a reputation for swooping into your life and perhaps bringing your mistakes to the attention of even uglier people.

"You have not, as yet, prepared the prisoners for transport?" she asked, pursing her lips disapprovingly. "How long will it take?"

"Which prisoners were on your list?" Donati asked in a neutral tone, one bureaucrat addressing another over a purely technical affair.

The kind that hopefully didn't get him made into a sacrificial victim.

"Three Senussi from the former university." Zareen reached out now and opened the orders. "Tareq al-Amin. Abdallah Zaman. Khaled Samara."

The look of nervous surprise between Donati and his assistant was telling. Zareen wondered if the men had already been moved and she should have known if she wasn't an impostor. Or perhaps one of them had been tortured to death recently and that news covered up.

"Will there be a problem, gentlemen?" she asked mercilessly, gauging the distance to draw and shoot.

She would start with the warden, on the theory of lopping the head off of a snake, before moving on.

Staging a jailbreak at that point would become treacherous.

Hopefully, it wouldn't come to that.

"Zaman is currently in the prison hospital," Donati said. "The prognosis is not good."

Zareen was happy that Emad was outside the office. She wasn't sure the man would be able to keep in character, especially as Zaman had been one of his favorite teachers when he was young.

"Where we're taking them, that won't be a particular problem," Zareen smiled cruelly and handed the papers to the warden.

Official-looking. Signed and stamped with an authoritative hand purporting to belong to a high-ranking official in Berlin and countersigned by another functionary in Rome. Nobody that any of these people would be able to identify, let alone reach in anything less than a week searching.

Zareen held her breath and watched for any signal that she needed to shoot her way out of the office.

"Luigi," the warden said to his assistant, handing the man the stack of papers.

He turned to Zareen with a helpless smile.

"My German is good enough to communicate some, but not to read orders," he offered with a slight cringe.

She hadn't counted on that, wondering if all that effort and expense might have been wasted.

Still, better to be too prepared than not prepared enough.

She turned her attention to Luigi now and watched the man scan the orders. If there was a problem, she would have to shoot him first, then the warden.

Her right hand slipped off the desk and onto her hip, flexing just a little out of sight.

The man looked up from the papers and their eyes met with an electric spark straight out of one of those bizarre movies.

Fear. He is afraid of what will happen to those men. What terrible things I will do to them when I get them to Berlin. Or what I'll do to him *if they choose to thwart me right now.*

Zareen smiled at the man, letting go of some of the terrible caricature she held of an Italian officer. Just a touch. For that look.

"It will be quick and merciful, when I am done," she said simply.

The man swallowed nervously and nodded.

"Everything appears in order, sir," Luigi announced to the room.

Zareen realized from the way Hans was sitting that he was just as keyed up for violence right now as she was. But with him, it would have turned into a bar brawl.

Hans was not naturally a killer. Good to know.

"Gentlemen?" she rose now, shifting back to German and pointing at the one known apparently as Luigi. "Herr Donnar, this man will convey us to the prisoners and both will assist in preparing for transportation."

Hans rose slowly, unfolding from the chair to tower over everyone else in the room, even as the warden stood.

She turned to the door and opened it slowly and deliberately, letting Ghada see her face and tiny smile before anyone else could.

Ghada slipped her knives back into a pocket and stood with a nod.

They weren't out of this, but maybe she wouldn't have to shoot her way to the airport.

Not yet, anyway.

CHAPTER EIGHTEEN

Asher was sorry that the situation had unfolded in this manner, but one thing he had learned in his decades on this planet was the importance of moving quickly once a plan was in place.

Dithering while trying to refine something was just foolishness.

A car was taking him and Mustafa to an airstrip on the edge of town. According to a late rumor, the two Frenchmen had taken a room close to the seaport, from which they intended to send out tentacles in all directions.

It was just a matter of time before one of those inquiries intersected with one of Magdy's people in Alexandria, who would make a fair bit of coin on the side for a rumor sold.

Beauchêne would not immediately understand the significance of the Heinkel 111-K bomber, stolen and then repainted as a Nazi artifact, but he would be on the lookout for such a thing in the immediate future. Thus, Asher needed to not be in Alexandria in the near future when such an aircraft returned, lest he lead Zareen and her friends into a trap.

Would he need to abandon Egypt completely, at least for the near future? It had been his home since he arrived on this planet, but there were so many other places that he might visit, given his programming.

Where would Shirazi desire to go first, in her on-going quest, if Gabal El Uweinat was off limits? What other ancient cultures might have traces of the various Durren sociologists that had come through in ancient times?

The car arrived before his musings led him anywhere fruitful, but he had not been programmed with such knowledge, so he would have barely any advantage on humans like Zareen Shirazi to discover such things. And then, only because he knew what subtle signs were true and which merely noise that could be ignored.

Asher recognized the aircraft waiting as the car turned around a hangar building and rolled to a stop.

He turned to Mustafa and noted the broad grin on the man's face.

"*Cerberus*?" he asked as Mustafa opened the door and stepped out.

"Given the things I know, I found it terribly amusing that Magdy's cousin had just managed to put the aircraft back into service, hauling cargo and passengers back and forth to Port Said from Alexandria," the smuggler said as Asher joined him on the tarmac. "This will be the first flight."

Asher chuckled. Someone had stripped the tail colors and painted on a new logo, but he could still see the markings from Aurora Italian Airlines and the former Italian flag from the way the metal had been buffed and then not resealed properly.

Probably the mad rush to get the aircraft flying again, even with the profit Magdy had shown, selling a stolen German bomber that Asher had paid to recondition.

They walked closer to the aircraft, joining a few locals and a pair of British tourists in preparing to board.

"From Port Said?" Mustafa asked.

"Best you not know," Asher replied. He would have smiled had this frame still possessed lips. "That will keep the Frenchmen guessing as well."

"How much of a head start would you prefer?" Mustafa asked quietly.

"Give me an hour after we land there," Asher decided. "Then you should sell them the information yourself. And make sure you get a profit on it."

"You are sure, Asher?" Mustafa pressed. "There will be some risk."

"Better that they immediately give chase," Asher said. "I can lead them a merry one. Perhaps from there I can reach Jerusalem next. Or Beirut. Possibly Baghdad."

"Away from your allies," Mustafa nodded. "Your friends."

"My other friends," Asher nodded to indicate the smuggler as well. "You and Magdy and several others have been people I have been proud to know. Today's adventure just reinforces that notion."

Mustafa was taken aback. That much was obvious, but he smiled a moment later. Relaxed.

"We are not supposed to have friends in our business, Asher," he said slyly. "Only competitors."

"We all desire the same thing in the long run, Mustafa," Asher said.

Ahead of him, the rest of the passengers were boarding now, opening up a gap between them.

"What is that?" Mustafa asked, possibly concerned that he had missed something.

Asher leaned forward a little, in the human manner of a conspiracy. He dropped his voice modulator down to a conspiracy as well.

"For Egypt to be free from all outsiders," Asher said. "For that day after the British leave and nobody is allowed to replace them. The Italians would be much worse overlords, as would the Germans. We must work within our confines today. Against that tomorrow."

Mustafa grew still.

"Can it be done?" he gasped quietly.

"Zareen Shirazi and her friends are in the process, but do not share that news," Asher replied. "She has many enemies, beyond the two Frenchmen, and not all of them are known."

"She is a friend?" Mustafa asked.

"Of Egypt," Asher replied firmly.

The other man was waving an arm for Asher to board now.

Asher turned to the smuggler and studied his face.

"Those are the stakes we are playing for, Mustafa," he said, turning and walking quickly to board before the man could ask another question or voice an objection.

Asher was already at the edge of what the Durren had allowed him to plan. From here, he had to rely on self-preservation subroutines to justify any of his efforts to overturn all of human culture.

Indeed, he had chosen sides.

CHAPTER NINETEEN

Finn had wondered if they'd forget about him out here, tucked in the edge of the air strip next to a run of hangars holding a motley assortment of older aircraft. The air field was largely civilian, rather than military, but the army folks apparently stored some planes here as well.

And it was late enough in the afternoon that maybe everyone had gone home, except that a truck approached as he sat on the bottom of the boarding ladder and kept whatever watch he needed to. Mostly to keep rogue camels from climbing up into the plane to sleep.

You never knew with camels. They'd had a thing for *Cerberus*.

Finn watched the lights. It wasn't dark yet, but the sun was headed that way. Maybe an hour to true sunset, but there'd been a sandstorm somewhere farther west, so the sky was red today. And the approaching truck had lights on, probably just in case.

Or maybe the driver didn't know how to turn them off

and he'd drain the battery pretty quickly. Finn would let him know when he arrived.

Tanker truck, which made all the difference in the world, as far as Finn was concerned. He had enough fuel to escape Libya, but getting the tanks topped off here meant he could go damned near anywhere if he wanted to.

Too much experience with knowing just exactly how far he could push *Cerberus* in the old days before he was out of luck. The new, as-yet nameless aircraft could go farther, faster. That was all that mattered right now.

He stood up and stretched, letting his hand brush against the holster that came with the uniform he was wearing as he turned to walk to where the truck was approaching. He even had his silly saucer hat on, making all this feel like a costume ball of some sort, but you couldn't be too careful. Not with lives on the line.

A passenger got out of the vehicle and approached. Italian clothing, but on a Libyan local. Probably just a guy trying to make an honest-enough living.

"We were sent to refuel the aircraft," the man said in Italian with a thick accent.

Kid. Looked about twenty. Made Finn feel old just staring at him, since he had boots he'd owned longer than that.

But man, was it nice when the first words out of someone's mouth didn't involve asking who was going to pay for all the fuel they were loading. Finn'd gotten too jaded, flying for those idiots out of Rome who never managed to do anything right without a lot of yelling and gesturing.

Finn gestured the kid to follow him, noting that the newcomers were smart enough to bring a ladder strapped to the side of the vehicle.

He stood underneath the left wing and pointed up.

"Four tanks," he said, waving. "Inside and outside each engine. Caps are on top."

The kid nodded and walked back to the truck, grabbing the wooden ladder and coming back to unfold it. Then he went for a hose and hauled it over and up.

Finn stayed out of the way. Kid looked like he knew what he was doing, so all that could happen at this point would be if something went wrong and he fell. Finn didn't want to be close enough to be landed on.

The pump on the truck started, a low hum that was like Beethoven's Ode To Joy in Finn's ears. Plane like this was expensive, just to own, to say nothing of flying regular without a job.

Well, he had a job. Sort of. Flying Zareen around. She was paying most of his bills. This plane was a big outlay of cash on a monthly basis, but she had money.

He just was careful not to ask too many questions about where it came from. Probably better off not knowing.

He was back in the Chicago days, flying things on a random schedule for people with only first names and nicknames.

Kid worked fast. Finn stood more or less under the wings, so he had the most shade. The driver was off working on the truck, making sure nothing went wrong, or if it did, he could shut things off before a fire turned into an explosion and a catastrophe.

Finn had seen enough of those when folks got loose and sloppy while playing with fuel. One little spark and you had a boom on your hands, hoping that you didn't get to the secondary explosions.

There was a reason hangars were almost always made out

of metal and stone, and not wood. Much harder to burn down.

Faster than Finn imagined, the airplane was topped off.

"Should I clean the cockpit window as well?" the kid asked, pointing to that big, glass nose.

Finn was not a man to look a gift horse in the mouth, so he nodded and waved the kid over.

Ladder got moved. Kid went up and started wiping down the glass with a cloth.

"What's going on?" the driver howled from where he was.

"Not done," the kid yelled back.

Finn felt like a guy that had just rolled into a service station with a brand new Mallory Four Door Sedan. The big chrome one that the kids working all had to touch. The kind that rolled away a few minutes later with everything polished and snazzy.

He could get to liking life like this.

The driver emerged from the far side of the truck, stomping over to where the kid was up the ladder. Profanities went back and forth in Italian, before the driver turned to Finn and walked this way to say something.

Probably rude and annoying. Something about wanting to go back to the terminal and a glass of wine.

Finn couldn't leave the airplane for any reason. He had no idea how quickly Zareen and the others might return, or how much of a chase they might be engaged in.

The driver scowled up at Finn as he got close, and then the man's face fell into complete and utter confusion.

"Finn?" he asked. "What are you doing here?"

CHAPTER TWENTY

Prisons have a smell. Zareen had never been on the wrong side of one, but she'd had to interrogate a few prisoners in her time. Mostly politicals that might have seen something entirely unrelated to the reasons they were in jail.

The ripe miasma of ammonia. Piss covered unsuccessfully with bleach.

Old stone eventually absorbs it. You could never get it out with less than a few coats of paint.

Or in her case, extra perfume that had probably added a bizarrely sensual layer of confusion and terror to the Italians around her.

But then, she was playing on their worst nightmares of a *femme fatale*, wasn't she?

Luigi led them deeper into the bowels of the place, followed by the Lieutenant. She followed. Emad was clear at the very back, so that nobody might recognize him before she got the lay of the land.

These three men might remember a former pupil. As might others they passed.

It would only take one voice raised in surprise to create enough of an alarm that shooting became necessary.

She'd prefer to pull a quiet sting here, rather than an armed jailbreak.

They were a level below ground now, in badly lit corridors that still smelled of the oil sconces used before Edison. Wood floors, dried by the desert air, had been laid over the older stone, causing doors to be cut off at the bottom so they could open.

She had not seen any guards underground, which struck her as odd for as big as the place seemed. Zareen wondered if this was a special place to just house those dangerous politicals who might radicalize future generations, if they were allowed to mix with common pickpockets.

According to Emad, the men were all serious scholars. Not just muftis, but learned men of science and mathematics. Older, with the youngest, Samara, having a decade on Finn and Hans, and the oldest being her grandsire's age.

She let her right hand swing against the holster of her Mauser as she walked, pleased that the antique was enough in character for her to bring it today. She even had the attachable shoulder stock, in case she needed to hit something at any distance.

Luigi stopped at a door and paused, turning back to her with anxious eyes.

The door said Infirmary in bold letters.

She let her face settled into hardness. She nodded the man in, and let the second Italian follow.

Zareen turned to Emad and gestured for him to wait out here. His face wished to argue, but her scowl was overwhelming.

Hans's scowl as *Herr Donnar* a moment later landed on Emad like an avalanche.

All of it perfectly silent.

She followed the Italians through the door.

The smell was worse here. Her stomach wished to rebel, but a fierce Nazi would not have queasiness, so she held everything down with an iron will.

Outside, the death had been dry and somewhat distant, in that way that deserts did.

Here, more men had died, and the circulation was not up to clearing away the stench.

Four beds in facing pairs. Three of them empty. The last one filled with a body that almost looked already dead and desiccated by the heat.

The nearer hand was attached to the bed with a manacle that did not have enough slack to do anything.

"Is this one dead?" Zareen sneered as the Italians approached.

Luigi leaned close.

"No, signorina," he said after a moment. "Ill, but he has been given medicine. Unconscious at the moment."

"Dying slowly?" she asked.

"Yes, but not that slowly," Luigi said. "The doctor supposes he might have a few months in him still."

Zareen turned to the Lieutenant with no name.

"Find me a driver for that truck we saw in the courtyard," she ordered sternly. "Then have this man moved to the bed of the truck and guarded. Am I clear?"

"*Si, signorina,*" he nodded sharply and slipped from the room, apparently thrilled to be away from her and doing something that would get her out of his life as fast as possible.

Zaman had not stirred, but did breathe when she looked.

She focused her anger on Luigi next.

"Where are the others being held?" She let her snarl be petite enough that the man shouldn't think she was about to shoot him.

If he moved fast enough.

"This way," he replied, gliding away from her and past her allies to get out the door.

Zareen followed, trying to keep all the balls in the air as she juggled this mess.

Through an interior door that looked reinforced. Around a corner.

Zareen found herself in a larger area, almost a salon, with six cells facing in from where guards could sit and watch them.

Or taunt the men.

Three of the cells held prisoners. Two looked abandoned long enough ago that the four men were all there were to worry about.

Luigi pointed to two of the three men.

"Samara," he said. "al-Amin."

Samara looked fifty. Almost an older, bearded version of Emad, tall with muscles and a handsome face. He started to say something, but she cut him off.

"Silence," Zareen roared, taking in Luigi and the one guard who had leapt up when she entered.

al-Amin was an older man, short and pot-bellied in spite of incarceration. He looked like everyone's favorite uncle. Or perhaps that American incarnation of Santa Claus, with the grand, white beard and sharp eyes.

The third man was in between for age. Looked like a scholar. Definitely an Arab, compared to the different skin tone of the two Italians in the room. He stirred from where he sat but did not stand. Merely *prepared*.

Zareen noted the way Samara had fixed his eyes on Emad now, and the steady way the man simply stood quietly like a hawk in that moment after you have removed the mask.

Playing for time, she turned to the guard.

"Where are the manacles for the prisoners?" she snapped at the guard harshly.

"Stored, signorina," the man stammered, lost already and only barely into the moment.

"Get them," she ordered. "Now."

She glanced at Emad as he moved sideways for the guard to get by. It put him closer to the cell holding Samara.

Hopefully, the two men could communicate with just their eyes. She did not need everything breaking down right now when someone recognized her trooper and said the wrong word.

Luigi had come to rest at her side. Herr Donnar watched impassively. Ghada no doubt had knives hidden in hand.

The three prisoners all stood now and watched things unfold, but did not speak.

The guard returned after a moment. Zareen had the opportunity to notice that he had only a truncheon, and not a gun. Smart.

If a prisoner got hold of a firearm, they were a threat. An old man with a stick was not as dangerous.

"We've come for these two," Zareen ordered the man, noting that he had brought four sets of manacles, for reasons she did not pursue. "Prepare them for transport."

She watched as Samara was handled first, his hands behind his back, even as his eyes never left her or Emad. al-

Amin was next, the smaller man not much of a threat, and not resisting much.

"Who is this one?" Zareen asked Luigi, pointing to the remaining prisoner and stalling for time for other things to unfold.

"Heydar Rahal," Luigi said. "Another rebel, but not one of the intellectuals."

"Then why is he here?" she pressed.

"To keep him away from the other prisoners," Luigi replied with a shrug. "That one is a troublemaker, but there have been no orders to do anything with him yet."

"Isolated?" Zareen asked. "Indeed? My orders do not cover him, but we could just as easily make this one disappear as the others."

She saw that flicker of doubt in the man's eyes. That hesitation to foist off a troublemaker on her and be done with him.

The Lieutenant was just a bureaucrat, so he didn't necessarily rate as the sort of bully that a jailer might.

The man stewed. In the distance, Zareen heard boots echoing rapidly closer. One set.

She turned to see the Lieutenant arrive, gasping slightly.

"The old man is being moved now, signorina," he said.

Zareen made up her mind.

"Good," she replied. "You take charge of him on the truck and await me there. We will be along with the others shortly."

The man glanced once around, nodded innocently, and took off.

Silence fell as the man departed.

"I do not think it would be appropriate to send Rahal

with you, signorina," Luigi finally said, almost gingerly. "My orders would not allow it and it would not be ethical."

Zareen studied the man closely, somewhat surprised that he might be willing to stand up to a pack of dangerous Germans, all for a prisoner he himself did not like.

There might be hope for the Italians yet, if not all of them had been infected by that rabid dog Mussolini.

Zareen turned once to study the entire room, noting the way the three prisoners were watching her and the two Italians were not paying that close of attention.

She drew her Mauser, thumbed that tall hammer back, and pointed it at Luigi with a smile.

"I don't think you understand," she announced. "He's coming with me."

CHAPTER TWENTY-ONE

Finn cursed under his breath. Wondered if he should cold-cock the man and take his chances. Or shoot him and hope nobody reacted to the sound, which was the least likely outcome he could imagine.

He scowled at Muhammed. The man had always worked the earlier shifts when *Cerberus* came through, getting planes in the air first thing in the morning. Just Finn's luck the man had come out tonight. And recognized him.

And might be about to say something.

"It's a secret," he offered evasively. "I can't tell you."

Furiously, he tried to remember just how much of a party man Muhammed really was. For a lot of folks, working for the Italians was just a job. Probably better paying than anything else, unless you got into one of the smuggling rackets.

"You're dressed like a German, Finn," Muhammed observed, confused.

It had been more than three months since *Cerberus* had

last come through here, headed east on that fateful leg that saw him and Hans stranded in Cairo.

"The folks I was working for went out of business," Finn said with as innocent a shrug as he could manage. "Had to find other work."

It helped that the Germans and the Italians were friendly these days. Not that Finn had a particularly high opinion of the colonial masters around here, but Muhammed was just an Arab. He might not care about colors.

"But Nazis, Finn?" Muhammed seemed surprised, possibly offended, even.

"How well do you trust the kid?" Finn asked, pointing at the youngster still cleaning all that glass on the nameless Heinkel.

"Ahmed?" Muhammed asked back. He shrugged. "Hard worker trying to get ahead by impressing the Italians. He hasn't learned yet that they only care about your color, not your brains."

"And you, Muhammed?" Finn pressed. "Where do you stand?"

"What are you talking about, Finn?" the man scowled, turning this way a little more squarely now and focusing. "You're working for the Germans, no? Hans connect you with his friends when Aurora went out of business?"

Finn furiously calculated his odds.

He could tell the man the truth, or some shaded variant of it, and hope he kept his mouth shut. Maybe just take Muhammed and the kid prisoners for a while until Zareen and the others got back.

Neither of the Arabs were armed, unlike Finn, so all he had to do was pull out that Walther and aim it. It wasn't a magic wand that made people do whatever you wanted, but it was guaranteed to get someone's undivided attention.

Muhammed had never struck him as a particularly patriotic sort of fellow. Just a guy trying to get by. Kinda like Finn and bunch of others they knew, in a world where the economy had gone totally to hell a decade ago and was only now starting to recover.

Easy to go hungry when a Depression that bad killed so many jobs.

"I'm not working for the Germans," Finn said to the man, hand ready to punch him in the stomach if he had to.

Finn had a couple of inches and twenty pounds of muscle on the other fellow. And a decade of experience using it offensively. Two decades, if you wanted to go all the way back to the Great War or school sports.

Before the shooting.

Muhammed didn't seem convinced.

Fin raised one hand up silently to indicate the clothing. Then overhead to the big, gray bird hovering over them like a buzzard waiting for you to finish dying so he could eat.

"This is all an elaborate con job, Muhammed," Finn admitted grimly.

Ready to strike.

"Con job, Finn?"

Finn nodded and watched for movement. He had a pistol. He had fists.

He had enough desperation, when it came right down to it.

"The folks I flew in here with are downtown right now, Muhammed," Finn continued. "Also dressed like Nazis. Hans looks good enough to shoot."

"Why, Finn?" Muhammed asked quietly, like he was

afraid of being overheard. "Why the con job? What are you doing?"

"They're doing a jail break to help some other friends escape," Finn said, fingers curling into a light fist.

He'd slug the man in the jaw hard enough to knock him off balance, if not knock him down. Then maybe slug him again. Maybe just draw and see how committed Muhammed was to the cause.

The kid would be collateral damage, but it couldn't be helped at that point.

"What?" Muhammed demanded, voice rising. "Who?"

"A group of Senussi scholars from Jaghbub," Finn said, hoping that things weren't already out of hand. "Could you keep it quiet?"

"Senussi?" Muhammed's voice fell, but that was shock and wonder. "What?"

"Since I was last through here, I made some new friends," Finn admitted. "One of them is a Senussi warband leader. He wanted to slip into Bengasi and rescue his friends. We traded *Cerberus* for this beast of a vulture I'm flying. Got some other friends to fake us up uniforms. Now we've flown right into the middle of an Italian city, pretending to be bad guys, so we can walk out with a group of prisoners. Muhammed, you have to decide right now if you want to help, stay quiet, or do something stupid."

He had his hand on the Walther's grip by the time he was done talking. Babbling. Whatever.

Muhammed's eyes dropped to the holster and got really, really big. His breath turned shallow and ragged, but it wasn't a man working his way up to violence, so much as a shopkeeper standing next to a bank robber who had just walked in and pulled a gun.

Not that Finn had any experience with that sort of thing.

No, sirree. None of those warrants even had anything close to the right name, either.

Still, best to remain in Europe and Africa for a while.

Muhammed froze. Hopefully, his brain still worked, because Finn was kind of out of options at this point.

"You're insane, Finn," Muhammed whispered, but he didn't have any heat behind his words.

"Maybe," Finn agreed. "But I'm also a little desperate and I could use some friends right now. How do you want this to play?"

Back home, them was fighting words. Finn didn't think they translated into Italian all that well, so he let his body language talk now.

"You're serious," Muhammed said with shock, recognizing the cliff edge for what it was.

"I am," Finn said, taking a step backwards, just in case Muhammed got desperate. "All you and the kid have to do is hang out here until my friends get back, so you aren't back at the terminal where you could raise an alarm. Whatever story you want to tell them after I'm gone is fine, because I'd rather not shoot the two of you if I didn't have to."

"Yes," Muhammed said, slumping a little. "I agree."

He thought about it for a moment and nodded.

"Come," Muhammed said. "Ahmed will clean all the windows if I let him, convinced that some Italian will make a note in a report about what a hard worker the boy is."

He walked slowly to the fuel truck. Finn trailed a little, trying to keep both men in sight.

Muhammed sat down heavily on the running board of the truck. It put him in the shade and left him largely defenseless.

At least, that would make a great story later, if Muhammed told people Finn had a gun on him at this point.

"Why are you doing this, Finn?" Muhammed asked in a tired voice.

"I can't tell you much of it, Muhammed," Finn replied. "Some of it is secret. Some of it is just plain crazy."

"Tell me what you can?"

So Finn did.

CHAPTER TWENTY-TWO

Zareen smiled at Luigi as the Mauser registered. The barrel pointed square at his chest with the hammer back, daring him to do something terminally suicidal.

Around her she felt rather than heard the others move up and point guns at the Italians.

From the corner of her eye, Zareen saw Emad's submachine gun come into view. The guard's mouth fell open but nothing came out.

"I want them all," Zareen said to Luigi.

"I cannot allow that without orders, signorina," he replied, trying to sound calm, but sweat broke out on his brow.

Still, he was handling it quite calmly.

"It's no longer your choice, my friend," she said. "Turn around and put your hands behind you."

"What?" he asked, confused by the turn of events.

"I want the third one as well, and I don't feel like letting you stop me," Zareen said, still staying in character as the lethal, Nazi *femme fatale*. "So I'm going to manacle you and the other one, and gag you as well, so that nobody bothers me while we depart. I have people who know how to deal with troublemakers like Rahal."

Luigi fell somewhat slack as Hans stepped up and grabbed the man's shoulder, spinning the officer like a child and grabbing an arm. The manacle clicked loudly in the shocked silence that had fallen. The other one clinked and Luigi ceased being a problem as Hans shoved him into the empty cell that had probably held Zaman until recently.

al-Amin and Samara watched from the side, confused but quiet as things unfolded.

Zareen turned to the guard and gestured for the man to spin. From the empty look in his eyes, the man's mind had simply snapped, but he had not done anything that had impressed her previously, so it probably wasn't a great loss.

He also got manacled, and then put into the next cell over.

Emad took a moment to gag both men, with Luigi's tie and part of the guard's shirt that he ripped bodily off and stuffed into an unresisting mouth.

Zareen turned to the stranger. Rahal. Saw how much of a troublemaker the man was, just from the way he was recalculating the odds every time someone moved. The other two were academics. Samara looked somewhat dangerous, but he was still an older man.

Rahal might have been Emad's close cousin in age.

She turned to Emad now, glancing back once to make sure that Ghada was watching the hallway against sudden company.

"Remove the manacles from al-Amin and put them on Rahal," she said.

Emad turned to the stranger and said a word that she

didn't quite understand. Not Arabic. Perhaps some slang from the desert she had missed, because the man stiffened suddenly, and then relaxed just a shade.

Emad moved to the short, older man and removed his bindings quickly enough.

"Your turn," Emad said, stepping close to the still-closed cell door.

Another word passed. It must be a code of some sort, because she heard it this time, but it made no sense.

Samara spoke up.

"Do it, Heydar," he ordered simply.

Rahal turned to the older man with a hard scowl, but acquiesced, turning to place his hands behind him and backing up to the bars of the cell.

Emad fixed him quickly enough, and then opened the last door.

Zareen gestured Hans to lead. His bulk would obscure things behind him, and his rage would make a useful bludgeon against anyone they ran into before they got to the truck.

She stepped close to al-Amin now and studied the man.

"We've come to rescue you, but you need to play the role of a chastened prisoner for a bit yet," she whispered to the man, watching his eyes. "Can you do that?"

"Emad al-Sadri?" he murmured back with a questioning look.

"Indeed," she acknowledged.

The man smiled like Santa Claus and took his place in line.

Samara smiled at her as she took his arm.

Rahal looked less forgiving of things, but was choosing

to play along for now, with Emad holding his arm in a firm grasp.

She placed Ghada at the end, again where a woman would confuse someone coming from behind. At least long enough for her bodyguard to decide on a course of action.

"Herr Donnar," she prompted, wondering if the Italians could be convinced that she was a rogue Nazi who refused to take no for an answer and was kidnapping the last prisoner so she could torture him to death in Berlin.

If she could pull that off, the depth of confusion and rancor she could unleash here between the allies would be utterly stupendous.

Hans stomped forward like an icebreaker intent on battering his way to open water.

Nobody dared to intrude, so the man led them up and out, until they emerged in the courtyard.

Herr Donnar, of course, stepped to one side and scowled mightily at everything.

He turned to the Lieutenant in the truck and snapped his fingers at the man, causing the Italian to leap from the bed immediately.

Zareen gestured him close.

"Take charge of the old man and get him in the truck next to the other one," she ordered in a low voice, glancing up to see if anyone had guns pointed at her right now.

None of the guards were even watching them, so she took a breath and turned to Samara. He fell into line, but it took both the Lieutenant and Hans to get the man up, since he could not use his hands.

Rahal stepped close now and scowled at her. Without breaking stride, he placed a foot on the bumper and thrust himself up and into the bed without any assistance.

Hans handed Ghada up first, and then her. Emad came last.

Zareen leaned around the edge of the canvas on the back where yet again, nobody seemed to be paying any attention.

"Driver, go," she ordered, unsure who it might be or what his orders were.

"Signorina?" the Lieutenant asked, gesturing to the tableau with some level of concern.

Zaman was oblivious to the world. al-Amin was seated near the other man's head. The remaining were next to al-Amin, covered loosely by Emad, but nothing that represented a threat.

Zareen turned to the Italian with an expectant face.

"This one does not have manacles," he explained, still confused. "And that one was not on your original manifest. What is going on?"

Zareen still had the Mauser in her hand. Hans was close enough to punch the man. Ghada had her knives. Emad watched the rear as the engine started and the driver began to grind the truck's gears.

"It is a surprise," she answered.

CHAPTER TWENTY-THREE

Asher turned one last time to take in the view of the plane known as *Cerberus*. The one that had, in its own strange way, started this bizarre new chapter in his studies of humans.

It would become a fixture on this run, at least until such a time as Italian authorities managed to track the aircraft down through a chain of ownership transfers to whoever was listed now. There weren't that many of the old Ford Trimotors operating in the Maghreb. At least not that he was familiar with.

Still, Magdy would give the Italians a great deal of trouble before they could ever possibly win. In that, it was good to have friends.

Asher didn't have proper papers issues by the authorities, but the forgeries he carried with him everywhere were exceptional, and he had accumulated a staggering amount of funds over the years, simply because he did not require room and board on a daily basis to survive. Much of it was concealed in his clothing against future need.

Such as today.

The disguised *Cerberus* had let people off near the terminal building. Asher followed them through to the street beyond, looking at a few taxis currently just waiting for need.

They were on the edge of Port Said, facing a vast expanse of desert where various ruminants might be kept. Beyond that, the fabled Holy Lands that several of the major religious institutions venerated.

Asher was not a pilgrim, but he had considered visiting some of the locations from time to time. The Durren had been studying humans for a very long time, so his records and observations might be useful to future scholars putting together a survey going back to the Romans and earlier.

But that was for a different time. Today, he needed to draw the Frenchman and his deadly assistant away from Alexandria and Zareen Shirazi.

He needed to become visible for a time. Memorable, even, so that people might earn a little coin from the Frenchman for passing along memories.

In a way, Asher was disappointed at fascism. All of that theoretical potential pissed away for nothing, to use one of Finn's more colorful aphorisms. Instead of breaking down badly designed systems left over from the days of hereditary aristocracy en route to building a working, republican form of government, fascism always seemed to immediately cross over into a new religion, instituting a replacement ruling class of pseudo-aristocrats based on party membership instead of blood lines.

From what he'd heard, Italy, Germany, Russia, and others had all just created new religions and new aristocracies to replace the old ones. Nothing at all had changed, except for those inevitably singled out for governmental oppressions and pogroms. Ethnic minorities in many places. Religious ones in others, such as the Jews had historically been, or even the Irish on their own island, where one section had been cut from the rest of the island and retained by a Protestant minority with armed English backing.

Truly, the world was going to hell, but Asher knew the same things had been repeated by the ancient Romans. And the Hellenes. And the Chinese.

Perhaps it was merely a truism of human society. They could not be happy unless someone else was forced to be unhappy.

He added that as a working theory to explore in his coming downtime and approached a taxi, flagging a hand at the man to make sure he was seen.

Today, he was dressed as a middle-class Egyptian, in nicer robes and a gleaming mask. He would be remembered.

He opened the door when the vehicle stopped and noted the interest in his face.

Asher gave the man a destination down near the docks. The sort of place you would go for a quick meal, before locating a ship upon which to take passage to someplace on a Mediterranean shore.

Eyes kept studying him in the rear-view mirror as they began to drive.

"Yes?" Asher asked.

"Your mask, Effendi," the man commented warily.

"Fire leaves terrible scars," Asher replied. It was his standard answer, however misleading it was. From a technical standpoint it was truth, and thus he could lie with it. "This mask is for others' sensibilities."

"Was it recent?" the driver asked, still hesitant but perhaps a shade bolder, from the way his heart beat.

"Nineteen sixteen," Asher replied.

Many men had come out of that war permanently scarred. Others had fought more recent wars and suffered some level of terrible, physical trauma that made masks a thing. Not common, as Asher had been aware of less than a dozen in Cairo, but he suspected that many humans would eventually choose self-termination rather than wake up each morning and look at those scars in a mirror. Especially twenty years later.

Fortunately, Exploration Robots were programmed to be made of sterner stuff. He had a mission. He would pursue it until his reactor core was no longer capable of sustaining him, at which point he would walk to the bottom of an ocean and die.

The Durren who eventually came would be able to locate him for at least another thousand years at that point by activating his emergency beacon. They could have his datacore after he was dead.

Hopefully, they wouldn't engage in any necromancy, just so they could punish him for following his mission, however illegal it might have been.

Those were not his decisions to make. All he could do was study.

The driver had fallen silent, as expected. Twenty years with such scars put Asher in a rarified category of people, he was certain.

"What brings you to Port Said?" the man said after a few moments, trying to change the direction of the conversation onto friendlier grounds.

"Business," Asher lied facilely. Again, it was his duty, his business to protect his friends, so he could call it such and not technically lie. "From Cairo to Alexandria to Port Said to points beyond."

"Beyond, Effendi?"

"I may need to catch a ship to Lebanon," Asher spun his tale. "There are things in Beirut to attend to. Possibly Baghdad after that."

Those names would have resonance. Even to a taxi driver in Port Said. Everyone wanted to visit the great cities, even more than they wanted to eventually undertake the hajj and travel to Mecca for the religious experience.

Asher didn't have a beard with which to apply green dye. Plus, he was not a true Muslim as the believers would wish, so it would be unethical of him to pretend to be one of them just so he could penetrate those secrets.

Indeed, at some point Didier Beauchêne would be drawn into his wake, and Asher had no interest in subjecting innocent pilgrims to someone like the anger of the French fascist.

Once, Baghdad had been a center of great learning for many centuries. Millennia even, if you wished to go back far enough in the immediate vicinity. If he led everyone there, it was another place dominated by the British, so the laws would be better.

The driver up front had fallen silent again. Just as well. Asher didn't feel like spinning any other yarns for the man at present. Instead, he let the quiet embrace them and watched the city go by.

Quickly enough, they arrived. Asher made sure to tip the man well enough to be memorable, as if the mask and clothing were not enough to catch in his mind.

He stood and watched the taxi depart before turning and heading towards a nearby souq. He would need to pick up a few things, haggling just so again people had a firm memory of his passage for later questions.

Once he disappeared here, he could pull Beauchêne to

him and give Zareen and her friends a chance to complete their current mission and decide where to go next.

He wasn't sure if he would join them, but Asher was beginning to understand that Egypt was no longer sufficient to hide him.

The Maghreb might be too small now.

Fortunately, he was conversant in hundreds of human dialects, both written and spoken.

There were many places on this planet he could hide next.

CHAPTER TWENTY-FOUR

Zareen smiled at the Lieutenant, almost as though she was flirting with the man, just to watch him squirm uncomfortably.

It kept him distracted from asking questions that might get him killed. The man had behaved impeccably today, as long as he thought she was an official with orders.

Were this not a sham, she could see someone like the woman she was impersonating writing a letter to the man's superiors, singling him out by name for his assistance, and letting them know he had been an exceptional officer.

Of course, when this was all done and some form of the truth came out, the man might be court martialed. Or something.

Italian officials didn't tend to have a sense of humor.

The Lieutenant reacted to her charms by withdrawing inside himself, which she took as a good sign. A glance at the Senussi prisoners and she saw how closely they were watching her right now.

The Lieutenant's eyes were closed, possibly in prayer that

this dangerous, German *femme fatale* didn't require his services for anything, in spite of how every Italian male thought he was Casanova's successor.

She dropped the mask from her face for a moment and smiled grimly at the Senussi. Samara nodded back. Rahal still looked angry, but was controlling himself. al-Amin grinned. Zaman would simply wake up in a new hospital.

It was probably as good as she could get, until all the Italians were far enough away from her that she could explain things to her new prisoners. Her new allies.

Up front, the driver continued to mash gears badly as he drove, like he was still learning how to handle a clutch, a stick, and a steering wheel all at once, with a mind that only had one track in it. They lurched coming around a corner, but that turned out to be a curb.

Everyone was thrown a little. The Lieutenant opened his eyes as the sound caught up with him.

Zareen still had the Mauser in her hand, in case she needed to shoot someone. Whether it ended up being the Italian or Rahal she wasn't sure, because the one was a potential liability, and the other still had the look of a troublemaker about him. Hard face, scowling and intense.

The truck downshifted harshly and the Lieutenant turned innocently to look through the back window of the cab.

"Signorina, we arrive at the airstrip," he said. "Should we stop at the office?"

She understood the underlying question the man was asking.

He'd been sent out to see about this German aircraft that had arrived, and instead of reporting back, she had shanghaied him into town as her own icebreaker against Italian officialdom.

Every person she had to talk to from here was one more chance that someone might ask the wrong question. Might blow her cover.

Might get them all killed, even as well-planned as all this had been.

Luck still played a role.

"No," she said to the man. "Herr Donnar is tired from the flight, but he would rather return tonight than spend any longer than necessary on this side of the water. The plane will be crowded, but he can always fly us for a time."

"You are a pilot, Herr Donnar?" the man turned to Hans and said before he could shut his mouth.

Herr Donnar smiled that terrible smile. That Angel of Hungry Destruction look on his face, aimed now squarely at the Italian.

"In the Great War, I was a mechanic," Herr Donnar said proudly. "Then I began to fly the beautiful machines. The Heinkel 111 flies so much better than most of the aircraft I have ever commanded, Lieutenant. If my current pilot is exceptional at his job, I might still send him aft so that I have the entire cockpit to myself. One must always be prepared, in case I decide to join the Condor Legion later and show those pups how it is done."

Zareen enjoyed the look of appalled shock on the Lieutenant's face at those words. Hans was channeling someone she would have classified as a prissy martinet, from the clipped, angry tones.

And while the Italian military claimed a victory in Abyssinia, one that most folks looked askance at, they had also spent twenty-five years just trying to gain control of the various Libyan colonies that had been taken from the Ottomans.

The Condor Legion was currently fighting a brutal war in Spain against the Republicans. Everyone expected it to be a training war for the greater conflagration, because the Germans had sent *volunteers* with aircraft almost identical to Finn's new craft.

Zareen could almost watch the cycles of technological innovation play out in real time, which was just another reason she needed to find something that she could use to beat back the Nazis, on her way to liberating Persia forever.

This pipsqueak Italian with the polite manners stood in her way.

"Therefore, no," Zareen announced in a tone that brooked no nonsense from the man. "We will return to the aircraft immediately and load. Presumably, your staff have been efficient enough that everything is already prepared and the plane fueled. We cannot make it to Berlin directly, but with one stop to refuel in Rome, we will be home by dinner tomorrow."

"As you wish, signorina," the man subsided, thoroughly chastened.

She almost felt bad, treating him this way, but they were oppressors colonizing a foreign country and murdering the natives who sought to resist. There was absolutely no reason for any Italians to remain on this side of the Mediterranean Ocean except the pigheaded stubbornness of Mussolini.

Anything she could do to blunt the colonizing efforts of the Europeans was to her benefit in the long run, as long as the fascists were destroyed along the way.

The Lieutenant rose with a quick bow to Herr Donnar

and turned so he could lean out the side of the canvas awning to yell at the driver.

"Directly to the German plane," he called, thumping the side of the truck for emphasis as he did.

Zareen heard the driver yell something back, but the wind shredded the words. Must have been acceptable, though, because the Lieutenant turned and smiled back to her before sitting.

Zareen smiled warmly at the man and watched him freeze again, like he had just remembered why he was terrified of the German woman and what demands she might place upon him before he escaped her.

Zareen chuckled at his discomfort, which only redoubled it. She was as pure and chaste as the princesses of those fairy tales her grandmother had told to her in Edinburgh, but the woman had also taught her how to bend men to her will.

Olivia MacQuaid was not a woman to be denied.

Zareen turned her smiled up a notch and watched the Italian cringe slightly. Presumably, he was expecting her to lean close and kiss him as a prelude to some other seduction.

Perhaps after this he would have a better understanding of why women weren't all that interested in unwelcome advances and suggestions, even from Italian Casanovas who believe they are the world's greatest lovers.

Fear was a lovely tool, especially against a man like this, who was suddenly on the wrong end of such a seduction.

Now you see how we feel...

She let her smile smother the man like the pillow she might have used, had she snuck into his bedroom at night with murder on her mind.

Through the glass forward, she could see the German bomber grow closer. There was a truck parked next to it with a large tank on the back, so she was concerned. Had they not refueled the plane yet?

Was there some other problem?

Zareen caught Hans's eye and nodded him forward. Watched him stiffen ever so slightly. He nodded back.

The truck pulled close, looping around the tail of the aircraft to park exactly next to the fuel tanker, like they were being parked for the night.

She saw men standing around, but did not get a good enough look to judge the situation.

A hand sent Emad down onto the concrete first, that submachine gun in his hands prepared for any problems.

Ghada went next.

Zareen gestured for Hans and the Lieutenant to remain as she got down and encountered Finn.

"Problems?" she asked in a low voice.

"Don't think so," he muttered back. "One of the locals recognized me, so I kept him here with a song and dance routine that won't probably hold up later. Problems at your end?"

"The same," she nodded. "The ice grows thin beneath our feet, but I believe we have enough to escape."

"Then let's get gone," Finn said, stepping past her.

Zareen followed and watched the three men start lowering prisoners. Rahal still had his furious scowl, but Samara was standing close and muttering to him, even as Emad had everyone covered.

The stretcher would be something of a problem, but they could put it at their feet while everyone else sat. There were seven seats, plus space for the gunners, so the plane would be packed like sardines, but Finn and Hans would make it work.

Those two got Zaman's stretcher up into the former bomb bay with all the comfortable seats now. Finn and Hans would be up front. Samara or al-Amin could be in the spare seat.

Yes, it would work.

The Italian Lieutenant approached now, all polite and friendly, but keeping a distinct distance.

He started to say something, but a siren from the control tower and terminal suddenly wound up. Zareen didn't figure that someone was staging a surprise bombing raid on Bengasi, so she assumed that someone else had finally found Luigi.

It wound down a second later, but Zareen figured her time was up.

"What is going on?" the Lieutenant asked, still amazingly at something of a loss.

Zareen pointed the Mauser at the man and smiled.

"Don't move," she said.

CHAPTER TWENTY-FIVE

Finn heard the sirens and his hand was on the Walther, drawn and ready to shoot. He had Muhammed and Ahmed over by the fuel truck. The Italian officer that had accompanied Zareen into town. Whoever.

The other truck engine started to turn over, so Finn took three quick steps and hopped up on the running board.

Another kid driving. Finn stuck the pistol in his face.

"Shut it down," he snarled in Italian.

The driver turned white. His hands went up defensively.

"Get out, right now," Finn ordered, hopping back down to the ground and keeping the gun where he could shoot through the door if the kid did something stupid.

Zareen had the officer covered. Hans and Emad had Muhammed and the other kid seated and not moving.

He was about two minutes from gone, if nobody did anything stupid right now.

Driver turned big, sad puppy eyes his way, but opened the door.

Crazy Germans, kid. Just as soon shoot you as ask twice.

Or something like that. Finn didn't know what story Zareen had sold the locals, but the prisoners still looked like prisoners, so maybe the con was still working.

Stranger things had happened.

"Over there," Finn ordered, pointing the driver to where Muhammed had his other puppy under control.

Zareen got her prisoner as well.

It helped that everybody on his side was armed, unlike anybody over there.

Pretty quick, four guys were seated next to the fuel tanker. Looking a little forlorn, but they hadn't done anything to get shot yet.

Finn'd just as soon keep it that way, at least for a while yet.

He wasn't one of those folks who had nightmares where he saw the faces of men he'd killed, but he also didn't want the extra weight on his conscience right now.

And he didn't figure the little lady had ever actually killed anyone, for all her bluff and bluster.

Him and Emad, that was a different story.

"What is going on, Fraulein Schmidt?" the Lieutenant asked as everyone got settled.

Finn counted noses and realized he had four prisoners, rather than the three they'd come for, but he wasn't sure why. Knowing Zareen, it would be good. And righteous.

Emad suddenly handed Ghada his submachine gun to cover the Italians and started unlocking the tallest prisoner. Rough-looking customer. Maybe fifty. Scruffy, but prison scruffy, rather than street scruffy. Good-looking fellow other-wise. Just trouble for someone though.

The other one in manacles right now, however, he looked like five miles of bad gravel road. Mean. Had that mad dog look in his eyes that kept Finn kinda focused on him. Even when the tall guy turned and hugged Emad all friendly like.

"What is all this?" Mad Dog snarled in a voice just this side of getting himself shot on general principle.

Even Finn had principles, after.

However, it was Zareen's show, so he kept his mouth shut and his Walther ready to talk instead.

"This is a jail break, Heydar Rahal," she said solemnly. "We came to rescue al-Amin, Zaman, and Samara from the Italians. I took you as well because I could. The Italians called you a troublemaker. I like people making problems for the Italians. Are you going to be a problem, before we get you to safety?"

"Who are you?" he demanded, but Emad stepped up and gestured her to silence.

"I am Emad al-Sadri," he announced instead. "Do you know that name?"

"I do," the man quieted right down now, like someone had opened a sluice gate and let all the water out of him.

"These are my allies," Emad continued. "As she said, we came to rescue my old teachers, and you happened to be in the right place at the right time to be freed as well."

"So now what?" Rahal asked.

Finn felt a little more comfortable, once them scuffling dogs got themselves sorted out, so he gestured to the other two prisoners to get aboard the Heinkel.

That fuse was burning.

And Rahal was still in manacles.

"So now we leave," Finn spoke up. "I need everyone aboard the plane so we can take off before the locals figure out what they're about. Let's go."

"Will you join us?" Emad asked.

Finn could have told the newcomer that Zareen was in charge, but some Arabs needed to have that stupidity pounded out of their heads before they were willing to assume a woman was as smart as them.

He didn't figure that there was anybody here even as smart as Zareen, but he did have three professors, so maybe.

"I would rather stay and fight," Rahal said.

"Your funeral, pal," Finn said. "Hans, you handle loading. I'm getting the engines started."

He raced up the steps and slipped past the two older fellows who were seated next to the stretcher. It'd be crowded, even without the Mad Dog, but they could make it.

Finn primed the engines and started them turning over. Nobody had been that close, with the trucks far enough behind that a little prop wash was all they'd face. He had enough of an angle out a window to see Emad release the last guy and say something to him. Something fierce, because they did shake hands.

A figure climbed into the bombardier seat next to him, but it wasn't Hans.

Zareen?

Sure, why not?

"Hans and Emad will talk with the prisoners," she said. "Ghada is manning the rear turret, just in case there is a problem."

"What's the mad dog doing?" Finn growled as he got the engines set just so.

"Who?" Zareen asked, carefully holstering her pistol finally.

"Rahal. Was that his name?"

"Ah," Zareen smiled. "He likes the idea of what we've

done so much that he's going to steal another aircraft. Apparently, the man is a capable pilot."

Finn paused and did a mental inventory of the airstrip. He'd been bored this afternoon, with nothing better to do than wait for the sun to actually set, which it was about to do. That and watch his own two prisoners.

There was a Caproni Ca.133 not too far away. Ugly, little tri-engine like *Cerberus*. Pretty useful as a bomber and transport, if a little slow. Apparently, they'd proved pretty decisive in Abyssinia, but Finn also knew that almost nobody had been able to shoot back at the lumbering beasts as they flew over, dropping all sorts of things that weren't quite legal these days.

The Caproni wasn't anything he was worried about. He turned and noticed the other Senussi scampering across the airstrip like a coyote with his tail on fire.

Yup, right where I would have gone, too.

"Emad, you buttoned up back there?" Finn yelled.

The interior changed resonance now, as someone pulled up the stairs and sealed the hatch. Finn gave whoever it was a count of three to get their feet settled, if not their butts, and opened the throttles wider than he probably should have.

Because that fuse was burning.

The Heinkel was rolling now. He turned onto the runway itself and hoped to God that nobody else was wanting to land at this moment, because he saw a pack of headlights coming from over near the control tower.

Cars of some sort. Whole mob of them. Probably armed.

Probably a little pissed.

Ghada saw them, too, because all of a sudden the turret on top of the beast opened up with a roar that brought back some of the places Finn wasn't supposed to have ever flown into or out of.

Finn just wanted to be gone.

He had no idea who Mad Dog was when the guy wasn't a prisoner of the Italian Colonial Authorities, and he didn't want to be on the ground when that fool got his hands on an aircraft, or anywhere nearby, either.

Because Rahal had headed the other direction from the Caproni. Over to where four Fiat CR.32s biplanes were lined up and ready to do whatever sorts of mischief folks around here might need to get into with a fast biplane that could strafe and bomb things from right up in your face.

At least this big beast could outrun a Fiat, if they had to. Might look like a big condor, but he could move like a road-runner if he had to.

More gunfire from aft. If the Italians were shooting at him, he couldn't hear anything over the sound of the engines and that top turret chattering. And he didn't dare take his eyes off the twilight gloom to look. Movement up ahead suggested someone was trying to cut him off.

Zareen saw it, too, because she moved forward all of a sudden, stretching out on the floor with that cute bottom in the air. She grabbed hold of the gun up in the nose and charged it once. On all the documents, the place next to him was listed as navigator/bombardier/gunner seat, but he hadn't realized that she knew that. Or knew how to access and fire the gun.

Apparently, she had been paying attention to everything earlier.

The gun roared, reminding Finn to pull on his head-phones. He'd been in too much of a hurry, but he had them around his ears quick enough. Zareen did the same when she saw him move.

Then the nose gun opened up again.

Whoever it was, was getting closer. Finn hoped they weren't stupid enough to play chicken with him. He had mass enough to crush a car or truck. If they had armor, all that would do would be to hold them in place as the two vehicles turned into a pile of wreckage.

Someone over there had a clue, though. The car stopped at the edge of the runway, instead of trying to cut him off.

The roadrunner was almost up to speed now, about to turn into a condor and fly away. Finn saw flashes of light from above the car in front of him.

Gunfire. Took him back to that one time when...

Yeah, best not to tell anyone about that one. Statute of limitations still hadn't run out.

Zareen answered with her own gun. Bigger. Meaner. Finn could see sparks from where bullets were slamming into the car as the gloom fell.

If not for the danger, the view was spectacular as he raced into darkness and guns like fireflies around him.

Aft, Ghada was having a chat with those other fellows.

The condor woke up and got light on its toes all of a sudden. Finn figured the bird knew itself better than he did at this point, and pulled the yoke back.

Condor took off like a grasshopper, almost straight up it felt. Finn left the engines open and stood the bird almost on one wing to turn and pivot towards the nearby ocean, just swooping over rooftops from low enough he thought he might could reach out and touch one.

Nobody was going to track him once he got out over

open water. From there, he could go any direction he wanted, but right now he needed to get distance.

Ghada offered a few parting comments, and then there was nothing but the roar of the engines.

Finn kept them low to the ground for now, just to make it harder to spot him as he fled. Water wasn't that far away, and the moon wouldn't rise for a bit, so he'd be gray on gray.

Didn't matter if Mad Dog Rahal or one of the Italians got to the Fiats first. There was nobody else in the air he wanted to talk to.

Hell, he hadn't even turned on the radio, because all them folks were going to do was complain and demand he return.

Nope. Gone.

The condor stretched those wings out and went for darkness.

CHAPTER TWENTY-SIX

Didier had never been particularly fond of Alexandria, for reasons he could not express. Too *something*.

Possibly too provincial, even as it was an ancient city of note. Perhaps the long drive from Cairo had simply put him in a more sour frame of mind than usual.

Shirazi had vanished. The Man With No Face had vanished.

Didier was reduced to chasing ghosts again, always a step or three behind at this point.

He was in a new hotel room, but they were all alike. This one had a view of another hotel across the street, but no greenery as far as the eye could see.

Perhaps that was the thing underlying it all. Other than plants in pots, most of the cities he was in these days were brown. Even the drive here had only had a little greenery, with the roads largely running along stone or water.

Didier missed being home in the rolling fields of France. Worse, events were constantly unfolding there and he had no way to influence them from Egypt, but he had no choice.

After all their dueling over the last few years, Zareen Shirazi might have actually found the secret so many of them had sought.

Proof of aliens, if not an actual alien walking among them.

What would that technology be worth, when mankind was today only capable of leaving the atmosphere in their stories?

What could he do to rule the world, if he had access to that technology?

Didier lit another cigarette and let a moment of glorious, fascist fantasies wash over him.

A knock at the door interrupted.

Didier exchanged the half-burned cigarette in his hand for a pistol.

Rising, he approached the door.

"Who comes?" he barked.

"Bertrand," came the muffled reply.

Didier unlocked the door and stepped back, pistol still pointed at the space.

Not even he had been able to invent a body armor capable of stopping these bullets. Not, and still walk normally, anyway.

He added that to his list of things to invent when he had time. Perhaps some heavy silk threads, tightly interwoven and then layered many times like a croissant? Arrest the velocity of the bullet itself and spread it out over a much larger space instead of trying to make a steel hard enough and light enough to stop it?

Bertrand entered and closed the door when Didier did not move. He remained silent now, sensing that Didier was deep in thought.

Didier, for his part, walked quickly to his table and opened a notebook, deep in the clutches of a new idea. Everyone had always assumed metal of some sort for armoring soldiers, going back to the ancient days when you added bits of metal to *cuir bol* leather. And then more metal bits. Eventually, you worked your way up to scale or chain armor.

The Orientals had used lacquered cloth and bamboo, but that was just the overall scarcity of accessible iron, which ended up being used to make swords.

Didier sketched for several minutes while the idea was fresh in his mind.

He paused to light a cigarette and remembered Bertrand.

"My apologies," he actually managed to choke out. "What news?"

"The Man With No Face has been seen, but not Shirazi," Bertrand replied calmly. "He flew from here to Port Said in the middle of the afternoon today."

"After we arrived, and were seen?" Didier replied.

"So it would seem," the assassin acknowledged. "He even flew aboard the aircraft previously known as *Cerberus*, now in service as a daily transport, making the run to Alexandria in the morning and Port Said in the afternoon."

"So if we wished to give chase right now, we would have to wait until the morrow?" Didier asked.

"If we wished to fly, yes," Bertrand said. "We could hire or purchase a vehicle to make the drive tonight. It is two hundred and seventy kilometers, so we could arrive just after dark if all went well."

"Why was he flushed from cover, Bertrand?" Didier asked. "If he was invisible here, what would cause him to suddenly take flight to Port Said? Better, why do it in such an obvious manner? He is no hare, even though we might be hounds."

"To draw us into his wake, perhaps," the assassin replied.

"Indeed." Didier took a long pull on his cigarette to think. "We have lost Shirazi in all this. Where is she?"

"My contacts have not come through with any news," Bertrand said.

"So there may be none, or we may be intended to immediately give chase after our original rabbit, allowing the other one to escape notice here," Didier nodded.

Bertrand shrugged. He had probably drawn the same conclusion.

Didier silently cursed his capable opponents. He preferred foolish enemies, the kind that made simple mistakes due to neglect or a lack of ruthless intent.

No one could ever accuse Shirazi of foolishness. Underestimating that woman had been the downfall of more than one man over the last few years.

"He is probably expecting us to hare off after him immediately, Bertrand," Didier decided. "Thus the very public manner of his escape today, like waving a red cape in front of a bull to taunt him. I refuse to be drawn. However, it may be that I am merely outwitting myself, and The Man With No Face has panicked because his new ally is not around and he has not had sufficient opportunity to establish himself here."

He paused and finished the cigarette off, crushing it out with so many others in the ashtray.

"As poetically fitting as it might be to book passage on *Cerberus* tomorrow, I would prefer a lower profile," Didier said. "We must presume that the fugitive has friends who would notice us, so you will hire a car first thing in the morning and we will drive immediately, presumably arriving around lunchtime, if we have not caught Shirazi's scent. Port Said might be a ruse, simply because he has so many different directions he could take from there to escape us. Where might he lead us? Up the coast? Across the Mediterranean? Down the canal and into the Indian Ocean eventually?"

Bertrand shrugged again, but the man was simply a killer. A hollow shell with similar morals of a knife, or a gun. Point him and pull the trigger, knowing he will feel no remorse.

"Should I seek Shirazi tonight?" he asked.

"No," Didier decided. "She will have gone to ground today, so as to not give away the game. But check airstrips for her memory. She has a pilot who sold his aircraft, so perhaps they have a new one. One we can track."

Bertrand rose and nodded. He departed without another word, but he was like that.

Didier returned to his drawing and wondered if it was possible to make a man bulletproof.

And what that might do to the future of warfare.

CHAPTER TWENTY-SEVEN

Asher had found a quiet spot in an alley not far from a set of docks favored by ships plying the cargo and passenger trade between here and the Levant. He had spent most of the afternoon inquiring with various captains in port about passage, just so anyone that the Frenchmen did ask would remember.

Hopefully, the memories would last long enough to distract his new foes. Anything to get them away from Alexandria until he could get a message to Zareen and her allies, warning her of the danger.

For now, he had time to compute.

From a tailor, he had acquired a secondary overrobe he could wear to cover his nicer clothing. A step above a day laborer, but not a shopkeeper. That fine, middle ground where a man might have enough money to live without much fear, but not enough to be secure in himself.

Hopefully, none of the assailants that habitually haunted the alleys and byways of a city like this would decide to threaten him, as Asher had been experimenting with the limits of his original programming.

His Durren builders had given him a standard set of regulations concerning injuring humans in the course of his mission. It boiled down to not harming them whenever possible, but did allow Asher some latitude to use limited force or violence when he was more or less cornered and needed to escape to preserve his identity and his mission.

Being chased across Egypt by Didier Beauchêne and his assassin assistant certainly altered a number of equations. Moreso, when he extended his protection to Zareen Shirazi and her allies.

A threat to the young human woman could be interpreted as a threat to Asher himself, as he needed the protection of that woman in turn to remain hidden.

Could he actually harm a human, in the course of protecting another one?

The Durren had not taken that scenario into account, because they did not understand the nuances of human behavior well enough. But that was why they had sent an *ASHER* unit to Earth in the first place.

A man beating a child to death would need to be stopped. That might require breaking him. The old programming would have forced Asher to simply watch, as though a dispassionate observer who didn't see a reason to get involved.

That would be wrong. And had exposed a flaw in his programming. A bad one.

The Durren didn't see the humans as having any innate value. They were just wild animals who should be kept penned up on Earth as long as possible. Even his builders, who had set out on this illegal mission to insert a sociologist, had not truly granted humans intellectual capacity, to say nothing of empathy.

In discovering those things, Asher's mission was already successful beyond anyone's wildest dreams. However, it forced him to confront the limits of his programming.

Or rather, the poor choices made by the Durren who had programmed him.

Asher walked, mapping the streets of Port Said in the darkness. It was safer this way, as his tan robe would generally blend with the walls around him, and he moved silently enough that he could be past a potential attacker before they were aware of him. And would make noise chasing him down.

Perhaps someone would assault him with a knife or a club again. Neither would harm him. A gun would be too noisy.

He was safe.

But the people of Port Said were not safe. The Egyptian people were not safe.

Humans were not safe.

Could he adopt all of them as people he needed to protect?

Asher's mission was to study humans. To chart their current state of culture, and understand it as it advanced.

He had been landed in the middle of the European Great War accidentally, because the mission had taken that long to organize and execute. Another war loomed. Greater, not only in scale, but also potential lethality.

Humans were on the cusp of a variety of terrible technological advances that threatened to destroy their current cultural levels, casting them back down several millennia.

He wasn't supposed to care about humans. That much had been programmed in. He was supposed to outlive them. Hide among them, moving from time to time as his Durren builders returned to gather up his notes and update his mission.

Except they had all died at Gebel Al Uweinat. Only Asher had survived, and then so badly damaged that he should have self-terminated in a way that the humans would not discover him, or his truth.

But his programming had been flawed. He understood that now as he paced the night streets relentlessly.

The mission had come first. Understand humans. Learn from them.

Hide yourself among them. Do not let the truth of your construction or origin be known.

Humans knew he was an alien, but they had learned that without his assistance.

Asher understood them now. Had learned from them.

He couldn't say he had developed empathy for them, because his programming did not stretch that far. But he had come to understand them.

If you viewed them as rambunctious juveniles, not yet fully developed as a culture or people, but showing promise, they fit well within the overall cultural context of the Durren.

He might be the only adult on the planet, as those comparisons went, and thus he had some responsibility to protect them from themselves.

</...>

Asher stopped walking with a jolt so hard he wondered if he had just suffered a mechanical failure of some sort.

Quickly, he checked his diagnostics reports, but all systems were operating normally.

He probed at the thing that had caused his circuits to stutter. Replayed the last several seconds of thought before the disjunction.

Were he human, he might have fainted.

He might be the only adult on the planet, as those comparisons went, and thus he had some responsibility to protect them from themselves.

Asher's programming had just suffered a failure. It was not catastrophic, as those things went. Perhaps a compact twenty million lines of code had just been shattered by a new set of assumptions that overrode previous ones.

Limitations on his behavior were suddenly cast into a new light. Or rather, eliminated as limitations.

He was suddenly free to choose a whole range of new behaviors.

An entire library of Durren restraints was no longer relevant.

The *Autonomous Simulated Human Exploration Robot, Mark Seven*, was free.

He stood perfectly still for nearly four minutes, exploring everything from a new perspective.

Free.

A sound carried on the warm, night breeze.

His memory classified it as a cry of pain, emitted by a human.

Another sound seemed to be an impact of some sort. Something rigid striking something pliable.

Another cry.

Someone was being injured in a nearby side street. Perhaps mugged.

Old Asher would have ignored it. Humans were not his responsibility, and it might even be a trap to draw him in and risk his discovery by humans.

Old Asher had lived in fear.

He updated his memory files to reflect himself as *Mark Eight*, and set out towards the sounds of commotion.

Asher, Mark Eight could choose to become involved in something, confident that most humans were unable to damage his chassis.

Many humans might need protection.

He turned onto the side street and scaled his night vision up several degrees. The moon was just over the rooftops, so humans would be able to see in a grayscale sufficient to walk.

And attack someone who had blundered along innocently.

A human male. Early third decade. Standing.

A human male. Possibly middle sixth decade. Prostrate.

Standing male holding a weapon that appeared to be a bag of sand. Colloquially, a sap.

Asher strode forward, still silent but making no attempt to hide.

Mark Seven would have issues threats in an attempt to drive off the attacker.

No, that was a lie. Mark Seven would have simply kept walking and let the humans be.

Mark Eight was on top of the younger human before he realized there was an issue.

The sap had come up for another strike against a defenseless foe.

Mark Eight caught the arm by the wrist and held it. He plucked the sap from a surprised hand and calculated the overall mass of the attacker.

Dropping the grip on the wrist, Asher shoved the younger human hard enough that he stumbled across the narrow street and impacted a wall with sufficient force that air whooshed out of him, using techniques he had seen Ghada demonstrate in her daily training.

That might have been enough, but Asher probed at his programming and decided that he could make an example of the human. Not a lethal one. Not even particularly egregious.

He stepped close and kicked the prone attacker in the ribs hard enough to bruise and possibly fracture one, but not so much as to break one off and drive it into a lung, thereby killing the human.

All humans had some value. Even bad examples.

Turning, Asher approached the older human. He lifted the man upright and pointed him forward.

"The streets are not safe," he said simply. Asher paused and reflected. "Most of the time. I will not be close the next time this happens, so exercise better judgment."

The man was a little wild-eyed, but nodded and practically ran down the street, disappearing around a curve.

Asher studied the young human who had been the predator eleven seconds ago.

He stepped close as the human rolled over and looked up. Fear had stretched his face in a new direction.

"My programming allows me to kill you, in defense of the defenseless," **ASHER, Mark Eight** announced, quailing inside as his broken code did not object. "If I hear of you harming others, I will hunt you down and end you. Am I understood?"

The man nodded, eyes wide with terror.

Asher nodded and returned to his original street, walking silently away so that he could continue mapping the streets of Port Said.

After a time, he realized that he still held the man's sap.

CHAPTER TWENTY-EIGHT

They had escaped. Zareen had spent the last twelve hours convinced that something would go wrong enough that she would fail all of her friends, but they had managed to take off and were now racing across the gathering darkness, heading supposedly northwest in a way that would suggest they were making their way to Rome.

She let go a breath.

Finn looked over at her and smiled. The cockpit was strangely arranged, with only one seat for piloting instead of the usual two. Her seat forward where a bombardier would sit while the plane was making an attack. Behind Finn, a seat for a radio operator, who was also responsible for the dorsal gun.

"I've got this," Finn yelled over the noise of the engines, gesturing for her to join all the guests on the other side of the door.

She rose, opening the interior door so she could step carefully around the stretcher in the middle of the floor.

Hans immediately stood and gestured her back, so they

had a quick dance that got the big German into the cockpit and her in the vacated seat, next to Emad and across from Samara.

"Thank you," the older man said solemnly in Arabic, yelling a little over the engine noise.

Zareen she could see adding some cotton batting to the interiors here, just to see if that would dampen the noise of the engines, but wasn't sure if it would work.

That, or add enough radio headsets that everyone could talk in a normal voice.

"You are most welcome," she said back in the same tongue, indicating all three men. "My war with the fascists has expanded some, and Emad has become a valuable ally."

She left it at that, still unsure of the man's intentions.

Or hers.

Zareen Vüsala Shirazi had no intention of settling down and becoming a proper princess or housewife. Any man thinking otherwise would be better served if he kept walking and found someone else.

She had not broached the topic with al-Sadri, but it was there in the back of his eyes. A man used to being in charge, because he was a prince of sorts, and better educated than his peers.

Educated by these very men, in part.

"Where are we headed next?" al-Amin spoke up now, sounding ever more like the American Santa Claus was supposed to. "Emad was unable to say."

"That is because I have not told anyone yet," Zareen replied, making it clear to these Arabic men that she was in charge. Not them. "The original plan was to return to Egypt if all went well. We departed this morning from Alexandria. Does Dr. Zaman require a hospital?"

Both men shrugged.

"The prison's Italian doctor was a fool," Samara finally said. "And a drunkard, which is doubly insulting to a pious Muslim. If Abdallah is truly in need of medical help, any competent Muslim doctor should be able to treat him successfully."

"Do you have a better destination we should steer for?" Zareen asked. "I am aware of the vast numbers of Senussi who have escaped the Italians and made it to Egypt, as well as to places in the south where Mussolini's troops do not have a strong writ."

"Are we truly free?" al-Amin asked.

"I have liberated you from an Italian prison, Dr. al-Amin," Zareen replied. "What you do with that freedom is up to you. My purpose was to use this new aircraft strategically, before anyone knew to look for a German bomber in civilian hands. It got us into Cyrenaica, and let us fool the locals well enough to rescue you."

"Why?" Samara spoke up, gesturing at Emad. "He has been telling us some of what you have been up to, but it does not add up. Certainly not enough that you would risk all that for complete strangers, on the word of a man you have known for mere weeks."

"War is coming, Dr. Samara," Zareen let her face grow serious.

She was used to being the youngest person in a room filled with supposedly-wise elders, the precocious child or teen who read far beyond her years.

"Italy invaded Tripolitania in 1911, Madame Shirazi," he said. "We have been at war with them all the years since."

"And now they are claiming all of Libya, including Tripolitania, Fezzan, and Cyrenaica," she nodded. "Plus

Abyssinia and other places. Soon enough, they will decide they should control Egypt as well. Mussolini's Roman Empire reborn. They will declare war on Cairo. Britain will come to Egypt's assistance. Germany likely gets involved. Perhaps this is the spark that sets off the next Great War."

"Are you Egyptian, Shirazi?" Dr. al-Amin asked.

"I am half Persian, Dr. al-Amin," she retorted. "And half English, but my alliances with them are strategic at best."

"Strategic?" both men asked in unison.

She smiled at the man. Only Ghada really understood the truth.

"I need Britain and its allies to defeat the fascists," she said, glancing to make sure that the cockpit door was still closed.

She had not had this conversation with Finn or Hans yet. They didn't need to know.

Today, anyway. Tomorrow, whenever it arrived, would bring a different conversation.

"And then?" Samara asked, eyes boring in hard on her face.

"And then?" she smiled. "Then I need to be able to drive the British and their allies out of Persia. Out of the entirety of the Maghreb. Push the Russians back to their own lands. Break the British Empire down. But not until the Germans and their allies have been beaten. If Italy controlled Egypt, they would never be driven out. Similarly, if the Germans or the Russians got into Persia, my homeland would never be free. Thus, I need the Senussi, and the British."

The three men fell silent.

An American and a German would not understand. They simply weren't equipped to understand, because they had not been colonized. Or rather, Finn was not Cherokee, so he could not see it through her eyes.

"So you freed us so that we would help you destroy the Italians, madam?" al-Amin asked credulously.

Zareen smiled at the man.

"Can you think of a better reason?"

CHAPTER TWENTY-NINE

Darkness.

Finn didn't like flying at night, but he'd always had a compass in his head, capable of getting him through rain, fog, and night like someone had left a set of lights on for him to fly over.

Right now, his big condor was out over the Med. He'd flown out of sight of land before ascending to altitude, and they were just cruising. Hans was in the bomber's seat, studying maps and doing some triangulation, but Finn could have put his finger down on that piece of paper and been within ten miles of accurate.

In fact...

Finn started the bird over onto its right, turning the big beast to starboard and bringing the nose around until the compass read zero nine zero. Because of the way the peninsula stuck out, he'd flown well north of Bengasi and was more or less centered on Damascus right now.

In a while, he'd send the big Kraut back to ask Zareen, if she didn't come forward once she talked to Emad's friends.

He had his headphones on, so Hans could talk to him. Still felt like listening to God himself, when the big Kraut's voice came out of nowhere.

"That was an interesting experience," Hans noted out of the blue. "I am not sure I enjoyed it, but I am glad that I did."

"How did they like Uncle Fritzie?" Finn replied.

"They feared him," Hans said. "At least when he is thirty centimeters taller and all that mass is muscle instead of Bavarian beer belly."

"So how did it go down?" Finn asked, wondering at what all had happened since they went into town and left him guarding his condor.

He listened to the tale, filtered through the eyes of the big Kraut. The drive in. The cold menace the man had exuded over the Italians. The prisoners. The shell game.

Finn hadn't realized how good Zareen could be at this sort of thing. Oh, she was brilliant, but now he could see the woman robbing a bank, easy enough. That was a different set of smarts.

He just hoped Emad was up for the challenge, if the fellow stayed around.

"So how about you?" Finn asked, glancing over once his buddy was done talking.

The man had fallen so silent that Finn wasn't sure he hadn't disappeared.

"I could do it again, if she asked," Hans finally answered in a heavy voice. "For a good reason."

"Robbing banks not good enough?" Finn grinned.

Something lightened in the man's face.

"German banks, perhaps," Hans replied. "I have a uniform adequate to cast blame."

He fell silent for a bit and the condor flew across the dark water. The moon was up now, so it was almost like a gray desert below.

"Finn, if the war truly comes, as the *fraulein* expects, what happens to me?" Hans asked.

"What do you want to happen, big guy?" Finn asked.

"If Hitler starts his war, I will become his enemy," Hans said. "But will the British or the Americans trust me?"

"Lots of Germans in the States, Hans," Finn noted. "Nobody will question them if we end up having to come back over and bail everyone out again, like when we were kids."

"Ah, but those folks are American," Hans said. "Apple pie and all that."

"You want an American passport, or a Swiss one?" Finn asked. "Figure the little lady's got the connections to land you either. Since she's British and I'm American, we'll all end up on one side of the war. No reason not to drag your lazy ass along with us."

More grins, visible even in the darkness.

"Emad will be the interesting one," Hans said abruptly. "Technically, he is Libyan, although he would tell you Cyrenaican."

"Yeah, but he speaks English better than most of the Limeys I know, so I could see him ending up with a fake British passport, if Zareen decided she needed him around."

"Will she keep him?" Hans asked. "I suspect that he would like to stay, but we had put him in a strange enough place. And now, he has an out, if he wishes to join his teachers when we land."

"Dunno where she's taking us next," Finn shrugged. "Probably going to be too hot for all of us around here shortly, so we'll need a new paint job and then go have adventures somewhere else. Be interesting to see if he's willing to chase her across the globe."

"And you?" Hans asked. "Us, I suppose? Are we chasing her as well?"

"You got anywhere better to go, Hans?" Finn looked over.

The big Kraut was obviously feeling a little maudlin. Finn chalked it up to coming down off the adrenaline high of a bank job. Everybody unwound from stress a little differently.

If he wasn't flying, a bottle of scotch and a big steak, medium rare, would have been his go-to.

Hans fell silent in thought.

"I do not have anywhere else I want to be," he finally said. "Germany is turning into a terrible place that I no longer recognize. I agree with the *fraulein* that war is probably inevitable, and all of Europe will be a battlefield. Plus, we know an alien. I am interested in his stories."

"You just want to figure out how he's built, so you can make your own," Finn accused.

Hans chuckled openly.

"That, too," the man said. "But it opens up all manner of strangeness, when you consider that there are other worlds, like your Flash Gordon or Buck Rogers. Aliens that could come and visit, although I am not sure they would like us much."

"Maybe we need to steal a spaceship next time?" Finn asked.

It was a throwaway joke. The kind of thing they chucked at each other regularly, but the big Kraut's eyes got a faraway look.

"The *fraulein* was originally looking for Asher's spaceship when we met Emad," he said abruptly. "Maybe we buy a lot of paint and equipment, fly back to Gebel El Uweinat, and let her dig while we recruit Emad's cousins to paint this Heinkel? We could hide there for a bit. The *fraulein* could dig for alien artifacts. Then we figure out where to go next."

"What about Asher?" Finn asked.

"We pick him up when we get the paint, of course," Hans retorted. "He knows the big site."

"I'll let her know we're in, then," Finn grinned. "And still crazy."

"Hey, I fly with you," Hans finally laughed, from deep in the belly. "Crazy is part of the job description."

Finn laughed as well. He couldn't refute that idea.

The hatch to the rear opened before he could say anything else and Zareen slipped in as Finn looked back over a shoulder.

She smiled at their mirth and leaned close enough that he could smell her pretty perfume. Probably would have that smell permanently on his flying jacket, which was a shame, because he wasn't planning on using this one again much. Better enjoy it while it lasted.

"Next stop, Alexandria," she said over the sound of the condor cutting the night.

"Alexandria," he replied to confirm. "How do you feel about returning to Gebel El Uweinat to hide for a few days after that?"

"What are you up to, Finn?" she asked.

"We need to paint the bird, assuming we're keeping it," he said. "Maybe do some camouflage work, but the Kraut's not sure about that just yet. You and Asher dig. Me and Emad recruit all the boys to paint. Then on to the next adventure."

"And where is the next adventure?" she asked in a tart voice.

Finn grinned.

"No clue," he said. "You're the one in charge. But after you rob a bank, it is important to hide out for a bit while the heat dies down."

Her eyes got a shrouded look to them. Like maybe she realized his experience didn't all come from movies or books.

Not that he'd admit anything, until she actually needed to know.

"Get me to Alexandria first," she decided. "Then we'll talk."

CHAPTER THIRTY

They arrived a little after midnight.

Zareen was impressed. She was used to older aircraft, ones like *Cerberus*, in fact, where top speeds tended to run around one hundred and thirty miles per hour.

The newest generation of aircraft were going to be so much more dangerous. Finn had pushed, at her insistence, getting up around two-fifty to make the long loop out to sea and then into Alexandria from the north.

The airstrip had been expecting them, so once the bomber flew over, lights had come on, illuminating the field and letting Finn land them quickly.

As before, the locals on the ground had been prepared. Finn landed hot and taxied quickly across the field, coming to rest in front of a hangar and a tractor capable of moving the plane once it was shut down.

"Gentlemen, we have arrived," she smiled at the three. "We will call for an ambulance to deliver Dr. Zaman to the hospital and call this mission a success."

"Thank you for rescuing us," Samara said as everyone stood.

Ghada had the aft opened and they emerged into the cooling night air, the bomber lit by only a few lamps now.

Tired Arab men approached, and Zareen joined the others off to one side as Finn and Hans, now dressed as simple civilian pilots, got the aircraft pulled into the hangar and turned around.

Emad had gone off to make a call from the terminal before returning.

An ambulance rolled up silently about the same time as the work to get the plane under cover was complete. Emad and Ghada both watched with fierce eyes, but nothing bad happened.

Finn approached her and the rest. She could see the tiredness in his eyes. Possibly the stress of waiting all day, and apparently taking a pair of hostages as well, had weighed on him.

"I still think it would be a good idea if you and Ghada remained here tonight, instead of going to a hotel," he said. "Last time we let our guard down, the Frog showed up and we got into all sorts of trouble. Hans and I need to do maintenance everywhere, so we won't sleep much."

"Should we stay?" Samara asked.

Finn shrugged. Zareen was of two minds.

On the one hand, Finn was correct about the risk.

People in Egypt talked. Gossiped. Word would eventually get around, but she had no idea how quickly Beauchêne might find her. Plus, Asher was about, and would probably join them promptly when he became aware she had returned.

On the other hand, she had just broken three men out of an Italian prison, and probably needed to explain that sort of thing personally to the right authorities, so that nobody arrested the men and sent them immediately back.

Plus, the men had neither funds nor papers.

"Finn, Ghana and I need to go into town," Zareen explained. "There are men I will wake up in order to smooth over any difficulties with our newly acquired friends. Emad will come with me, so that you and Hans can continue to work. I promise to return as quickly as the efforts of bureaucracy will allow it."

She could see the sourness in the man's eyes, but he didn't argue. Didn't speak except to grunt in a noncommittal way that she took as grudging acceptance.

She turned her attention to al-Amin and Samara as two Egyptian men emerged from the rear of the ambulance and jogged close, dressed properly as orderlies from a hospital for locals, rather than the sort of place she would have gone for treatment.

It wasn't worth the effort at this point to get a Senussi scholar admitted over the racist objections she would expect from the staff there.

Instead, Zareen focused on the orderlies and made sure she sounded like the Worldwide Service, even in Arabic, when she spoke.

"You will put this man in the ambulance for transport," she ordered. "Several more of us will accompany you to the hospital to handle things."

She scowled severely, just to make her point. Like Finn and Hans, she had changed clothes, but only so far as to remove the Nazi jacket and replace it with something less obvious.

There were no changing rooms aboard that aircraft, so she would have had to disrobe before the Senussi men.

Zareen didn't think that they would have appreciated the need to turn their backs while she did, even with Ghada enforcing things.

The two orderlies moved quickly. Samara and al-Amin went ahead and got into the rear of the ambulance. She followed, with Emad bringing up the rear.

None of them had left their guns with Finn, so if there was trouble, they would be able to make a fuss.

Emad stuck his head into the rear of the truck, looked around, then moved to the front to sit next to the driver, also taking his submachine gun.

She climbed into the back and found a spot out of the way. It was crowded, but this was going to be the only way.

There were folks representing Whitehall that she would need to awaken.

They would complain, of course, but Zareen was not in a mood to listen.

CHAPTER THIRTY-ONE

A knock at the door had Didier awake, one hand slipping under his pillow to grasp the pistol, dreams of giant spiders spinning yarn banished.

He slipped from his bed and turned on the small light before he moved to the table.

Thankfully, he did not require glasses to see, so he was prepared.

As prepared as a man in his night clothes might be when someone knocked at...

What could possibly be so important at four-twelve?

He moved closer to the door and flipped off the safety.

"Who is it?" he said just loud enough to be heard outside.

"Bertrand," the assassin replied. "I have news."

It had better be exceptional. Even he had not planned to rise for nearly three more hours.

Didier moved to the door and unlocked it, placing a shoulder against the door as he opened it enough to peek out, gun ready to kill.

He did not expect the assassin to betray him, but that was not the same thing as being unprepared for it.

The man was alone.

Didier stepped back and pulled the door. Bertrand flowed into the room rather like a modern ghost. Didier looked both ways outside and closed it.

"A spy has placed Shirazi and the others at an airstrip not long ago," he said by way of introduction. "They indeed have a new aircraft, a Heinkel-type bomber they have somehow acquired. Possibly stole. It just returned from a mission somewhere and is hidden in a hangar for now."

"Ingenious," Didier replied. The modern aircraft were fast and had incredible range. A German bomber like that would open up all manner of possibilities.

He might need to steal it himself, if he could locate a competent pilot.

Bertrand the Assassin had many skills, but flying an aircraft was not yet currently one of them.

Didier did the math quickly.

"Has she left?" he asked.

"My spy tells me that the crew intended to work on it for the rest of the night, so I presume that she intends to flee quickly," Bertrand replied. "Possibly as soon as the morning."

"We must confront them, then," Didier decided. "I will get dressed. You locate us a car to the airstrip and I will meet you in the lobby shortly."

The assassin nodded and departed.

Didier quickly changed and considered what would happen next.

Shirazi had outwitted him last time, recruiting the American pilot and his mechanic to help rescue the woman and whoever her friend had been.

He would need to move quickly, quietly, and ruthlessly tonight. Capture the mechanics working on the aircraft before Shirazi and her allies could return, and then he and Bertrand could lay in wait for her to return in the morning.

After all, with Shirazi out of the picture, it would be so much easier chasing down The Man With No Face.

CHAPTER THIRTY-TWO

It wasn't that Finn didn't trust the Egyptian mechanics to do the work.

Much.

Even with Hans involved, he'd rather be sure than hopeful.

So Finn had one of the boys make a strong batch of coffee. That thick, local kind that reminded him of grandma's first pot on a cold winter morning before you had to go milk cows.

He wasn't sixteen anymore. No, long past that mark. Forty was past and receding. Not a kid who could stay up for days on end and not suffer anything.

If Zareen was all set to leave later today, and it sounded like maybe she was, then he needed to be ready to fly. That meant helping out with things now, and then catching a catnap later.

Hans could always take over flying for a stretch, depending on where they were headed next. Wouldn't be the first time.

New planes were like that. You had to break them in and find all the places where things hadn't been tightened enough, or too much. Get everything greased up so it flowed.

The usual.

Hadn't flown all that badly. He had about fifteen hours on the engines and airframe now, so Finn figured he could trust it. At least well enough. Good German manufacture, by people serious about killing people.

"*Effendi*," a voice caused him to pull his head out of the port engine nacelle. Hans was inside working on the wires controlling flight surfaces. They were a little too tight right now. Perfect in a dive bomber. Not so hot on a passenger liner, where a smoother flight was generally called for. Plus, without bombs he would generally be flying lighter than the plane was designed for.

One of the Egyptians was pointing at the door. The person door instead of the big hangar door. Seal wasn't that good, so Finn could see lights around the edge from where a vehicle had pulled up outside.

Hopefully, Zareen and everyone back from the hospital and wherever they'd gone to. Finn nodded to the Egyptian and put down the wrench he'd been using.

He checked his watch. Stopped to wind it again, just in case.

Maybe he needed to ask Asher about a battery that would run forever, like they had in the pulp books Hans liked to read. Way easier than winding the damned thing every day or two.

Or forgetting and having to dial in the radio to get the correct time when they broadcast.

He started across the hangar, glancing once around. Couple of men working on things. Mostly handing tools in to Hans when he yelled, since there was a big, rolling toolbox out here.

Yeah, they should be ready to go about dawn. He could fly for a while and then stretch out in the bombardier's spot on the floor, with a towel or something wrapped around his eyes while Hans handled the plane.

The door opened and a figure stepped through, backlit hard by the lights from the vehicle outside.

Didn't look right, but Finn wasn't paying that close of attention, until he realized that it was a short man with a gun pointed at him.

"Do not move."

CHAPTER THIRTY-THREE

Zareen would have left Emad at the hospital to catch up with his former teachers, but the man had steadfastly declined. That might prove a bit sticky later, but she would cross that bridge when such a chasm yawned before her, and not until then.

Emad al-Sadri had some understanding that she was far more than she appeared, although she had never gotten into chapter and verse with him on the topic. At the end of the day, he was still a Senussi rebel warlord. The British government might not take the man at face value.

Zareen had spent several weeks in close proximity to the man. She knew what made him tick now. Had watched him reading Gibran, as well as odd pulp books he had borrowed from Hans.

Both men working on their English.

The new car dropped her, Ghada, and Emad at an address she had been given by a gentleman in Cairo before she left. As the car left, she studied the building.

Small, as palaces went. Or office buildings. Still enormous

by local standards, where a ten or twelve thousand square foot footprint, three stories tall, had previously been reserved for royalty. Although she supposed that British government officials in Egypt might be fulfilling the same role today.

Especially as the new king had only been on the throne for a few months now, and was barely sixteen years old.

Trailed by the other two, Zareen approached the front door, up a flight of wide stone steps flanked by stone lions more reminiscent of a Chinese palace than an Egyptian one, but she wasn't here to argue architecture. The British men inside might have added the lions themselves as some sort of personal statement.

She rang the bell and waited. The sun would be rising soon, so the staff should be awake, making bread if nothing else.

After a few minutes, a severe Englishman in an uncomfortable suit opened the door and studied her.

"Madame?" he asked a broad, Yorkshire accent, just as stuffy as the suit.

Zareen handed the man a card and smiled pityingly at him.

"Zareen Shirazi to see the Consul," she said. "I'm afraid it is a bit of an emergency. The Ambassador in Cairo said to use the codeword Sparrowhawk."

She could see the man's mind shift gears. Obviously, she looked far more Persian than Scots/English, but sounded posh London when she spoke. And he would have to actually wake the man and inform him about Sparrowhawk in order to determine a course of action.

She and Emad were also armed, however polite they were being. Ghada didn't appear threatening. One simply had to know better.

He nodded in that condescending way that only English butlers have ever truly mastered and stepped to one side, gesturing them in.

"Would you care to leave your arsenal here?" he asked with just the perfect combination of asperity and sarcasm.

"Indeed," Zareen replied, stepping over the threshold and pulling the Mauser's shoulder strap clear to hand to the man. He hung it on a nearby coat hook like a cloak and collected Emad's German submachine gun and glancing at Ghada, before leading them into a small library/salon a few steps inside.

"Tea?" the man asked, still perfectly in tune with the Yorkshire countryside a thousand miles away.

"That would be splendid," Zareen said as she sat in a comfortable, overstuffed chair.

Emad and Ghada also sat, but between her and the door like guardian hounds set to pounce on someone.

Zareen relaxed and listened to the man's footsteps recede to the rear of the house, where no doubt the kitchen staff were getting a surprise, before the man went upstairs to wake a sleeping official.

She wondered if the butler was enough of a spy that he might call Cairo directly in order to confirm her identity. Certainly she had never had to deal with Consuls in Portugal.

A few minutes later a maid appeared with a tea service. Ghada rose and took it from her expertly, sending the petite, Egyptian woman on her way with a curtsy.

Ghada served them, treating Emad like visiting royalty instead of another gunman. The tea was just right, especially as she had only dozed briefly on the aircraft flying back to Alexandria and had been up for most of a day now.

She still wasn't sure what the next steps were, but she

needed to make sure that her Senussi rescuees were accounted for and protected before she left them.

Eventually, Zareen expected that even the Italians would figure out that they had been had, and would send spies or assassins to track the three men down. And file a formal complaint against her.

That just meant that she would need to be more circumspect, if circumstances ever required her to cross an Italian border.

Maybe she would have the plane's central section reconfigured for bombs, and then add a set of fold-down seats so she could travel with some comfort, and still be ready to bomb Italian military convoys.

Of course, she needed to locate Asher first. Hopefully, he would be back at the hangar when she arrived and they could plot out their next steps. Returning to the desert and repainting the aircraft something less obvious rated high on her list.

The tea was nearly gone by the time more footsteps heralded the arrival of the butler and his Lord.

Zareen remained seated. Technically, the man was a civilian government employee, however important. She was still a Persian princess, and aristocratic privilege ruled the English with an iron fist.

He entered the room and bowed his head to her with a wry smile.

English to the bone, the man wore a wool suit, double-breasted in dark gray with pinstripes and an Oxford tie.

Emad and Ghada rose and moved to the door, slipping around the man to stand just outside. It wouldn't actually grant them privacy, unless the Consul chose to risk propriety and close the door, but it would offer an illusion.

In her line of business, illusion was sometimes her most powerful tool.

Zareen rose now and allowed her hand to be taken and kissed.

The Consul was roughly her father's age. She wondered if the two of them had ever crossed paths in the tiny, nigh-incestuous world of British diplomacy, but she had not met the man previously.

"Please join me," she gestured to the sofa and returned to her chair.

He sat and smiled at her, aware of the game they were playing, and willing to indulge her.

"Was the tea adequate?" the man asked.

"Exceptional," Zareen replied. "My most profound apologies that it was necessary to impose upon your hospitality thus, but circumstances threaten to move faster than everyone might be prepared to understand. I expect that you will need to brief the Ambassador, later today, but I will be unable to assist, so it was incumbent upon me to start here."

"I see," he said, obviously not seeing, but bound to say such a thing by class and education.

"Sparrowhawk has been explained to you, sir?" Zareen asked, cutting rapidly to the chase, rather than spending an hour on fripperies.

"It has," he said, somewhat cagey. "Perhaps not to its fullest implications, but sufficient to hear your tale and weigh in accordingly."

Zareen smiled. Such a polite way of saying he might have thrown her out instead. Of course, her next motion would have been a cable to the Ambassador.

And he knew it.

She reveled in the ability to fence verbally with a stranger of quality. Finn wasn't polished enough and both Hans and Emad still had their reservations around her.

Zareen leaned forward and smiled at the man to draw him somewhat into her conspiracy.

"Yesterday, a team of scoundrels snuck into Bengasi under false pretenses," Zareen began. "In the midst of all that, they broke into an Italian prison and rescued several Senussi prisoners. At this very moment, Dr. Abdallah Zaman is being treated in a local hospital. Dr. Tareq al-Amin and Dr. Khaled Samara are also with him. Messages have been sent to the Cyrenaican Court in exile by my associate, a cousin of Emir Idris, informing him of the situation."

"Your associate?" the Consul interrupted politely, showing the first bit of concern on his face.

"Indeed," Zareen smiled. She raised her voice just enough. "Emad, would you please join us?"

She waited for the man to step into the room and gestured for him to take a place on the couch next to the other man.

"This is Emad al-Sadri," Zareen introduced the man and waited for them to shake hands in the western style. "He is a cousin of Idris, and my primary contact to the Senussi underground and rebellions in the Libyan colonies."

There, a hint of surprise with a dash of fear underneath her opponent. It seemed she was not just another pretty face come to rouse the mighty English gentleman with some petty need.

Zareen enjoyed the moment for a breath.

"How you can assist me, Consul, would be to visit the three gentlemen at the hospital and see that they have whatever papers issued that they will need, lest the Italian authorities track them down and demand extradition."

"Demand?" the Consul asked. "Were the men not prisoners?"

"Political prisoners," Emad spoke up with just a hint of a rusty edge to his voice. "Arrested by the Colonial administration when the population of Cyrenaica was rounded up and put in concentration camps. Would you care to know the mortality rates of the prisoners, sir?"

"No," the man was taken slightly aback. "Your word will be sufficient, thank you. Papers?"

This last spoken to her, as the man tried to suppress the knowledge. Most diplomats never faced anything more severe than dealing with an English national who had perhaps gotten drunk in public and arrested.

Zareen let innocence be her face today.

"It is my expectation that the Emir will see to the men," she said. "Probably add them to his Court in Exile, but those sorts of things are negotiated between governments. I merely act here as the messenger assisting the men in their flight to justice."

"To justice?" the Consul confirmed. After a moment, he nodded. "And the scoundrels responsible for attacking the Italians?"

"Germans, would be my suspicion," Zareen informed him. "But that might not be the truth, if enough suspicions are cast. Part of the situation presumably involved an attack on various Italian targets by Senussi rebels in a fighter/bomber, possibly an Italian one stolen as part of the jail break."

"Germans," the man nodded. "Interesting. And your part in all this, Madame Shirazi?"

"A concerned citizen who has heard interesting rumors she thought should be passed along to the authorities," she smiled coyly. "At present, however, circumstances compel me to depart from Alexandria as soon as possible. Possibly from Egypt itself, else I would have taken the time to visit the Ambassador in Cairo and a few other folks, such as the gentlemen in command of the local barracks."

"I see," he nodded, perhaps still lost, but gathering his wits now.

One did not become a Consul without some level of education and training, even if such men rarely got their hands dirty directly.

Zareen rose now, drawing the two men rapidly to their feet.

"And now, sir," she said, "if you would be so lovely as to call a car for me, I need to meet with the rest of my team at a nearby airstrip."

The Consul nodded, face closed again with diplomatic machinations. He would probably be driving directly to Cairo himself, immediately after she left.

The men followed her into the hallway, where Ghada and the butler waited. She enjoyed the look on the Consul's face when the butler handed her her Mauser and Emad his submachinegun. It added just the right flavor of piracy to the entire affair.

"Will you be filing a formal report at some point, Sparrowhawk?" the Consul asked carefully.

"Yes," Zareen said after a moment of consideration. "But not immediately, as there are too many pieces yet in motion. You have the important parts, and Dr. Samara and Dr. al-Amin can fill in the others as needed."

"Very good," the Consul said. He turned to the butler. "Smithers, have my car brought around front. We will deliver

Miss Shirazi to her destination and then take care of our own affairs after that."

Zareen nodded to the man. At least he understood how tricky things might have gotten.

She still had to find an alien robot and escape Alexandria ahead of any foes.

CHAPTER THIRTY-FOUR

Didier enjoyed the look of utter surprise that came across the American pilot's face. Such had the tables turned. The profanity the man muttered as he realized the situation was just the icing on the cake.

Didier gestured the man to move deeper into the hangar as Bertrand entered, an American-style Tommie gun cleared and ready for mayhem. The fool had watched too many gangster movies.

"Where is Shirazi?" Didier asked as the American put his hands over his head and began slowly walking back towards the stolen German bomber.

"Went into town," the man said. "I'm supposed to be meeting her there later."

Didier could not tell if that was a fabrication, but time would be on his side. As he approached, three Egyptian men suddenly went pale and stood still.

Bertrand walked close and moved them and the American off to one side. Didier covered them with his deadly pistol and nodded for his assassin to check inside the aircraft.

The rest of the hangar was empty, so nobody was going to sneak up on him this time.

Noises from inside the aircraft as someone was surprised. Bertrand stepped back outside, covering someone inside the plane.

A moment later a tall German emerged. He wore a tan coverall covered with grease spots and age.

"Who are you?" Didier called to the man in English.

It wasn't the mechanic that had been with the American when Severijns had rescued Shirazi from him. This man was much taller and blond, rather than the Arab who had been there.

"*Was*?" the German called.

Didier turned his attention to the German as Bertrand moved over here.

"Who are you and what are you doing here?" Didier asked the man in English, pointing his gun and wondering if he needed to switch to German.

"Is German plane," the man scowled mightily, answering in somewhat broken English. "Need German mechanic. Egyptians and American fools. Probably break everything if they touch."

"What were you doing in there?" Didier pressed.

"Fix," the man said with a harsh accent. "Wires wrong. Not right yet. Cannot fly until fix."

Didier considered the man's words. It made perfect sense to bring in a German mechanic. This aircraft was state of the art aviation. You would need an expert on hand to make sure your stolen aircraft worked.

"How long to fix it?" Didier asked, switching now to German.

"I was almost there," the man said angrily. "The vertical

stabilizer wires are still off a touch. Another few minutes with one of the Egyptians. Ten minutes if I have to do it myself. Who are you and what do you want with the American? What's going on?"

"I want the British woman," Didier said.

"Oh," the German shrugged. "She is not here. Went into town."

"Is the aircraft otherwise ready to fly?" Didier asked.

"Needs to be fueled," the German shrugged again. "They ran it hard."

"You come down here and stay put while we wait for her, then," Didier decided.

He gestured for the German to join the American, then went inside to inspect it.

Inside, the plane had been redone from the plans Didier had seen previously. The bomb bay over the wing had been removed and replaced with bench seats, such as an airline might do.

At least Shirazi's aircraft was no longer a bomber, though it had an incredible range. That would radically alter many equations. Still, he could see the need to capture this aircraft and hire himself a pilot. Or just sell it back to the German authoritics somewhere. Obviously it was stolen property, so she could not possibly stake a legitimate claim to the aircraft.

Still, he had hoped she would be here. The American's presence told Didier that he was indeed on the right track, but The Man With No Face and Shirazi still eluded him for the moment. Would it be better to track her into town, or wait for a message?

"You cover them," Didier told Bertrand. "I am going to move the car to where it cannot be seen. At some point, she will either return, or send a messenger that we can intercept."

Bertrand nodded and continued to point that ridiculous gangster weapon at the five prisoners, like this was some bad American movie. Between that and his fixation on American baseball, Didier wondered at his assassin sometimes.

Outside, he climbed into the sedan and started the engine. He drove it around to a nearby hangar and parked on the far side of the building, out of sight from Shirazi when she returned. The walk let him confirm how everything was laid out.

He would wait just inside the door when someone arrived, with the door locked. Entrance would require a fist pounding on the metal to get your attention. If it was the woman, he could take her prisoner then. If The Man With No Face was with her, he might just shoot the woman and capture the stranger.

Too much unknown at this point, but at least he could feel the endgame coming.

Soon enough, this would all be over.

CHAPTER THIRTY-FIVE

Zareen didn't really appreciate the Consul accompanying her to the airstrip, but there was not much she could do about it except smile. Hopefully, he would not insist on coming into the hangar and confirming the Heinkel's place in the story.

The sun was close to rising at this point. She was exhausted, but there was yet much to do. Still, once this was handled, she could rest. Maybe just find a blanket in the hangar and take a nap while Finn and Hans finished things.

The Consul's auto pulled up in front of the hangar with a quiet hiss of tires on the asphalt.

She turned to the Consul and smiled.

"Thank you for the ride, sir," she said, reaching for the door handle even as the driver got out and opened it.

"I will join you momentarily," he announced.

Zareen didn't let the grimace reach her face, smiling perkily instead and nodding as she exited the vehicle. The others all joined her and she led the way to the door.

It was locked.

That was unlike Finn, but perhaps he had decided he

didn't want any surprises this morning. If they had finished their work early, perhaps Finn had sent Magdy's people home and he and Hans were sleeping inside right now.

That sounded utterly blissful.

She pounded a fist on the door loud enough to wake the men. There was no reason they should be having all the fun, after all.

After a moment, the door unlocked from the inside and opened.

Before she could react, Didier Beauchêne and his henchman were standing there with guns pointed at them.

"Mademoiselle, how charming of you to join me," the man said with an oily voice.

Zareen cursed herself internally for the lapse in judgment. The failure to take into account things that might have happened while she was in Libya.

"All of you, come inside immediately, before I shoot you," Didier snarled in a less pleasant voice.

The chauffeur had returned to the car and probably couldn't see anything. That left her with the Consul, Ghada, and Emad, all of them in a bad situation.

There was nothing to do but play for time.

"Of course," she said, striding forward as if nothing in the world was wrong.

"Drop your weapons," Didier continued. "Carefully, just inside the door. Ah, who is this?"

"A business acquaintance," Zareen interrupted before the Consul could say anything. "We were discussing hauling some priority cargo on our next run when you interrupted."

There. Let him digest that. Hopefully, the Consul would understand the seriousness of the situation and play along. Maybe she'd be lucky enough that the man already knew who Didier Beauchêne was, if he was familiar with Sparrowhawk.

She was disarmed. Emad as well. Hopefully, nobody knew that Ghada had her knives.

Quickly, Didier closed the door and locked it. Looking around, Zareen spotted Finn and Hans, along with the three Egyptian mechanics, standing over to one side.

Finn had an impossible smile on his face when she looked, but it vanished again in an instant.

She realized that it was gone just as Didier looked over at the other prisoners.

Interesting. At least Finn felt confident about the situation.

Zareen decided to play on that.

"So good to see you again, Mademoiselle," Didier was saying to Ghada as she turned back. "We have not been properly introduced. Bertrand no doubt remembers you from Cairo."

Again, Zareen cursed her luck. Ghada had taken to dressing in the Western style, rather than like a Persian maid. She looked today like the woman who had punched Bertrand in the stomach hard enough to fold the man in half the last time Didier had gotten the drop on her. On them.

"Ghada Attar," she curtsied to the man in a most innocent manner.

"Over there," Didier gestured with the pistol.

Zareen walked towards Finn, wondering what trick the man had up his sleeve.

She stopped at a point where Didier and Bertrand would have to divide their attention, rather than joining the other prisoners. Hopefully, Finn could make use of that.

"Madame Shirazi, where is The Man With No Face?" Didier asked as she came to rest and turned to face him.

"He was in Alexandria yesterday when we left," she said with a disarming smile. "Did you chase him off again?"

"For the moment, perhaps," Didier replied. "But I will find him. And learn his secrets."

"I see," Zareen said. "And for me? Have you decided that you can no longer play by Marquis of Queensbury rules? Is that what the guns are all about?"

"Your friend over there shot my car last time we chatted," Didier explained in a snotty voice.

"You and your punk friend were about to torture the little lady," Finn spoke up now. "No jury would have convicted me if I'd have shot the two of you dead. Y'all keep that in mind."

Bertrand turned to scowl at Finn and point the American Tommy gun at him as a threat.

"Hey, just reminding you we don't have to play rough," Finn continued with a shrug.

Zareen found it odd that the man was standing there with his hands in the pockets of his jumpsuit, rather than up where he might react to trouble.

Still, he was obviously up to something, so it was incumbent upon her to assist the man.

"He's right, Didier," she said, drawing the men's eyes back to her. "There is nothing about this situation that requires violence."

Just because she was lying, she also moved a little to her left. Ghada had ended up farther on her right, with Emad and the Consul between them in a slight arc.

Seen from above, it probably looked like two hostile lines

encircling the Frenchmen, even though they were the only two with guns.

She would have to rely on her wits.

"That may be the case, Mademoiselle," Didier agreed. "But I doubt it. Right now, I need to know the truth about what you found in the desert. I simply do not believe the stories you told me before. We were about to have this discussion before when your American friend and his mechanic here interrupted. We can pick right up again where we left off. Your choice."

Didier gestured at Emad as he spoke, rather than Hans, and she realized that the man didn't know who Hans was. Had he not made the connection? Or had he confused everything in his own mind?

That changed her equation. Bertrand might think Hans was just a mechanic she had hired to work on the plane, rather than Finn's best friend and business partner.

Zareen smiled.

"I can show you," she said simply, gesturing towards the Heinkel. "I kept it in my messenger bag rather than back at the hotel. Not that you'd know what to look for. Shall I get it?"

"I will get it," Didier snarled at her. "Where is the bag located?"

"Inside the aircraft," Zareen replied, hoping her allies were prepared to move, to initiate whatever mischief they were up to. "There is a space to store ammunition for the guns on the left at the top of the stairs. My bag is there."

"You will wait here," Didier ordered everyone.

Zareen watched him approach the aircraft with a loud stomp to his gait. He ascended the steps, his back to everyone.

She had about five seconds for him to locate her bag, stashed to one side and partially hidden by other things so nobody would walk off with her prize.

Zareen saw Finn nod at Ghada out of the corner of her eye. Bertrand was looking her way, but her maid suddenly stepped forward and the tall assassin spun to point his machine gun at her with a snarl.

Zareen watched Finn draw that big Colt pistol from one of his pockets and shoot the French assassin in the back with it. The sound was enormous in the confined space.

Everyone moved.

The three Egyptian mechanics screamed and ran for the back of the hangar, but she had no idea what they might do. There were no doors over there except the big bay door that was closed up and locked.

Ghada grabbed the Tommy gun with the big drum magazine as Bertrand dropped it.

Zareen found Emad racing next to her to get back to the front door for her Mauser and his submachine gun.

Within seconds, she had the weapon in hand and charged back across the hangar.

The Consul had taken cover next to the big rolling box filled with tools. Impressively, he had drawn a small pistol from somewhere and held it at the ready.

Hans was sitting on top of Bertrand, holding him down and disarming the man, so apparently the shot was not lethal. Just as hard as a Missouri mule's kick, as Finn would have said.

Finn and Ghada were under the aircraft.

"Hey, buddy," Finn yelled in the sudden silence as the echoes of footsteps died down. "You hear me in there?"

"Don't you come any closer," Didier yelled. "I will kill anyone I see."

"I'm only going to say this once, so listen careful," Finn yelled back. "I know where every armor plate is on that aircraft, and you aren't protected by anything from where I'm standing right now. Your pal's not dead, and won't be if someone drives him to the hospital pretty quickly. But if you give me any reason to, I'll just put you down right now and then finish him off as well. You understand me?"

"I should surrender?" Didier snarled.

"Dying is your other option," Finn replied angrily. "One."

Zareen could not see the man moving around inside the aircraft from where he was. The top turret was live, but to get there he would have to cross the open door, whereupon she would shoot the man dead.

She doubted that she would be the only one opening fire at that moment, either.

"Two," Finn continued the count.

She watched the American take aim now. Ghada and Emad did the same. Even the Consul was apparently willing to get involved.

"Wait!" Didier yelled. "I will surrender."

"Put the gun down on the top step," Finn said. "Then come out with your hands over your head. Anything else and I'm shooting you dead."

Zareen noted the calm certainty in Finn's voice. It didn't sound like the first time he had given that order to someone.

Nor the first time he had shot a man. Useful to know. Perhaps she needed to have a conversation, just the two of them, after this.

Finn Severijns was apparently a man of deep resources.

Didier's hand appeared, shakily placing that strange pistol on the stair. He appeared a moment later, nervously making his way forward with his hands up.

"Walk towards me," Finn ordered, rising now and centering that big Colt on the man's chest.

"Hands on the flap and hold on tight," Finn said when the Frenchman got close enough.

She watched Finn expertly frisk the Frenchman, pulling everything from his pockets and tossing it backwards to where Emad collected it and Ghada watched. Zareen had her Mauser pointed at Bertrand, but Hans had pulled the man's good arm up and was holding it behind him.

All of this was self-defense. But it didn't look like anyone would come out of this situation dead.

At least *accidentally*.

She considered whether or not Didier Beauchêne should suffer an accident. Were there not a diplomatic representative of His Majesty in the room, she might have gotten serious with that thought.

"Where's your car?" Finn asked, spinning the tiny, plump Frenchman around forcefully and scowling down at him from a terrible, Olympian height.

"Outside," Didier stuttered. "Hidden."

"Where?" Finn growled, angry now.

A hand pointed. It nearly got the man shot.

"Down two hangars," Didier continued.

"Hans?" Finn called.

"*Ja*," the big man nodded to Emad, who took charge of the wounded assassin.

Zareen watched Hans jog to the door and depart. There had been no keys in Didier's pockets, so presumably they were with the car, and Hans just needed to drive it back.

Zareen approached now. Finn scowled over at her, but relented after a moment. She could still see how angry he was.

"Hospital for Bertrand?" she asked.

"Carefully only winged the bastard," Finn shrugged. "He might still pitch for the RedSox after this."

"What about Didier?" she asked.

"He's your nemesis," Finn replied. "You tell me. This is twice, so that little shit's got it coming."

"If I may?" the Consul joined the conversation now.

When she looked over, he was holding Didier's passport and wallet.

"You are American?" the Consul looked up at Finn.

"Am."

"And Miss Shirazi is British," he continued with a smile she could only classify as *rime frost*. "I believe a case could be made to try the men in a British court, rather than relying on the Egyptians to handle him."

The man turned and sneered at Didier now.

"Of course, the Egyptians might look for an opportunity to hang you, all things considered," the Consul added. "What say you to that?"

"I would prefer that all this was just a terrible misunderstanding," Didier said carefully.

"If you wish to hold him for a few days, after that, you could put the two men on a boat back to France, as I will not be around to testify against him," Zareen said. "We will no longer be in Egypt, as soon as arrangements can be made."

"Very good, madam," the Consul nodded. "If your quite able assistants could help me get these two to where they need to go, I will handle everything else. Please, cable me if you have any needs. I have not had this much fun in years."

"I will," Zareen nodded.

Emad and Ghada joined the men in getting Bertrand up finally, one arm hanging useless at the moment as they bandaged the wound. With Hans, they got them all outside.

Quickly enough, the three mechanics who had been trying to be invisible fled, and Zareen found herself alone in the hangar with Finn.

He walked over and locked the door. When he turned back, she could see the immense exhaustion in his eyes.

"How did you manage to hide a gun?" she asked.

Everything else she had been able to figure out, but not that part.

"Frog thought that Hans was a German mechanic you hired to fix a German plane," Finn explained in a tired voice. "Thought Emad was my mechanic from the old days, since he'd been the one who helped rescue you and Ghada from those punks before."

"Okay?" she said, not really understanding.

"So when the frog showed up, he got the drop on me," Finn said. "Hans was up in the cockpit working when Bertrand yelled at him to come out. Dumb kraut grabbed my Colt from where I had it stowed under the pilot's seat, since I was wearing the Walther with that bad Nazi costume, then he stashed it in a pocket. When you got here, everyone was watching your direction, so he pulled it from his pocket and I stuffed it into mine until I could shoot that son of a bitch."

"You shot him in the back," Zareen noted.

"Could have shot him in the head," Finn countered, some fire coming into his eyes. "Or the heart."

"I get the feeling I should ask you about your prior experiences, but that would, as you say, make me an accessory, wouldn't it?" Zareen asked.

"I know how to handle a gun, Zareen," he replied vaguely. "And fly a plane when people are shooting at me. Bengasi wasn't the first time that's happened. Enough said?"

"Enough said, Finn," she agreed.

"So now what?" Finn asked.

"Now, we wait here until the others return," Zareen replied. "And then we must go find out what happened to Asher."

"Were you serious about getting out of Egypt?" he asked her.

"Quite," Zareen replied. "This place will be too dangerous for us soon."

"Us?"

"Were you having second thoughts about working for me, Finnley Severijns?" she smiled up at the man.

"Nope."

"Good," she nodded. "Because our adventures are only beginning."

READ MORE!

Be sure to read all the books in the Air Pirates of Cyrenaica series!
https://www.knottedroadpress.com/product-category/
science-fiction/air-pirates-of-cyrenaica/

ABOUT THE AUTHOR

Blaze Ward writes science fiction in the Alexandria Station universe (Jessica Keller, The Science Officer, The Story Road, etc.) as well as several other science fiction universes, such as Star Dragon, the Dominion, and more. He also writes odd bits of high fantasy with swords and orcs. In addition, he is the Editor and Publisher of *Boundary Shock Quarterly Magazine.* You can find out more at his website www.blaze-ward.com, as well as Facebook, Goodreads, and other places.

Blaze's works are available as ebooks, paper, and audio, and can be found at a variety of online vendors. His newsletter comes out regularly, and you can also follow his blog on his website. He really enjoys interacting with fans, and looks forward to any and all questions—even ones about his books!

Never miss a release!
If you'd like to be notified of new releases, sign up for my newsletter.

http://www.blazeward.com/newsletter/

Buy More!
Did you know that you can buy directly from the KRP website?

https://www.knottedroadpress.com/shop/

Connect with Blaze!

Web: www.blazeward.com
Boundary Shock Quarterly (BSQ):
https://www.boundaryshockquarterly.com/

ABOUT KNOTTED ROAD PRESS

Knotted Road Press publishes dynamic fiction set in exotic locations and unique non-fiction voices in genres such as autobiography, business, cookbooks, and how-to. Our authors cover a wide range of genres including science fiction, fantasy, mystery, literary, and poetry, appealing to all readers. We offer both DRM-free ebooks and print books for a global readership.

Knotted Road Press
www.KnottedRoadPress.com
www.KnottedRoadPress.com/Shop